UNTHOLOGY 1

2010

UNTHANK BOOKS

First published in 2010
By Unthank Books
www.unthankbooks.com

Printed in England by Lightning Source, Milton Keynes

A CIP record for this book is available from the British Library

Any resemblance to persons fictional or real who are living, dead or
undead is purely coincidental.

ISBN 978-0-9564223-1-6

Edited by Robin Jones and Ashley Stokes

Cover design by Ian Nettleton and Dan Nyman

CONTENTS
- UNTHOLOGY 1 -

Introduction

- The Editors -

In 2001, on the publication of his *Complete Short Stories*, JG Ballard said that the reason he had written far fewer stories in the eighties and nineties was because the market had 'dried up'. It wasn't just that the magazines that habitually used to carry stories had ceased to be or had stopped publishing them. According to Ballard, people had 'lost the knack of reading short stories...They feel—when they buy a volume of short stories, if it's slightly on the slim side—they're somehow being cheated. They want a big fat read, represented by a novel—they've lost the knack and...it's a great shame.'

Nothing to cheer up JG occurred in the subsequent decade. The market for short stories has contracted further. Publishers refuse to publish short story collections by anyone other than the very well known (we have to go back to Helen Simpson or Will Self's debut if we're to think of a writer who made his or her name on the back of short stories). The spread of the Internet as a means of publishing stories has done nothing to expand their scope, specialized fiction sites seeming to prefer very short stories that can be read quickly like blog entries. These stories often seem like overdressed anecdotes or marginally evolved pub jokes. Outside of magazines specialising in genre fiction, like *Crime Wave* or *Interzone*, or competition anthologies the short story can often seem like a poor relative included under sufferance in poetry journals. Constraining the short story to a one or two thousand word limit (what Ballard would call 'a tiny little squib') often produces what seem like protracted poems, all glittery surface but with no room to manifest a greater sense of significance or surprise. The longer story, the story unafraid to chase a few clouds, to play with chronology and form, the story that might have some semblance of plot-drive risks dying of neglect.

Unthology is an attempt to reverse this trend. *Unthology* has no word count limit for submissions and no formal agenda. In accordance with the Unthank Manifesto we tend towards the unpredictable and the unconventional yet we're not ideologically opposed to the two thousand word domestic story or the short, sharp slice of life. We only ask that a story make us think and make us feel. Here, we've assembled seventeen pieces: fourteen short stories, two novel extracts and one piece of life writing. Some of these writers are veterans of the small press scene; for others this is their first time in print. All of these writers, though, in discrete ways, we believe, write stories that no one else could conceive. They ask questions, as all good stories do, about how we live now and who we think we are. To ask these questions is the knack in writing a short story if not the knack needed to read one.

.

Extract from Doing it by the Book

- Viccy Adams -

It was cheaper to travel by coach, but I'd walked to the wrong station. I remember the ache in my arms from carrying my case so far already. After the woman at the ticket desk had told me that the coach station was the other side of town, it seemed like a good idea to take the train. I had with me a handsome red leather suitcase. Spanish leather. Brass fittings. My initials next to the catch. Good, solid workmanship. I'd had it for years; it was an engagement present from one of my wife's relatives. It had been part of a set, but she took the other two when she left; one for her, one for our son. I had that suitcase for five or six times as many years as the marriage lasted. It was an excellent piece of work. Not like my wife with her restless feet and tendency to unravel into tears at the slightest provocation.

There was a train just waiting there for me, on the platform next to the entrance, and it was going my way. The woman at that ticket desk said, 'Hop on, sir, and you'll be home before you know it.' My suitcase wasn't light, and I'd already walked a fair bit because of going in circles with those bad directions the woman at the B & B threw at me. She didn't care where I went, so long as I left. Bitch. The ticket desk woman looked concerned for me so I paid up and I hopped on.

It wasn't an empty train, not like today. Full of people going from one place to another, and taking the train not the coach because they were in such a rush to get to the next place. I got on the quiet coach so as I could nap a bit on the way home. At first I sat down in a good seat, a window seat and in sight of my beautiful red suitcase. But some person made me move because it was their allocated seat. So I stood up and walked along and if my legs weren't so tired I could have cut them off, I don't know what I was about. Finally there was a seat that I was allowed to sit in. It was a bad seat, by an aisle and surrounded by scowling young boys and feckless parents with loud children. But it was better than standing.

Oh and it felt good to sit down. I remember, it was the last peace of mind I was ever to have, sitting in that seat with the weight off my terrible feet, and the promise that there wasn't far to go. I fell asleep. The sound of trains still remind me of my childhood and travelling to school; I used to fall asleep every day on the way home, listening to the lullaby of the tracks. That was when I lived with my family, in my family house, and I was only very young. I fell asleep then because the day had been so long and full of new, important things that I could not wait to dream of them. Also, sleeping made the next day come faster and the cycle would start all over again, and there would be more, more, always wanting to see more. This time I fell asleep because I was so very tired; I didn't care so much about learning by then, only about remembering. It was stuffy as well, with the windows closed and the heat of so many bodies packed in. I put my wallet into my jacket pocket so that I could sit more comfortably and put my jacket over my lap. I took out my book but I don't remember reading a single word from it.

When I woke up, I had forgotten that I was on a train, see, and it was not pleasant. There was a boy beside me, who was listening to music in headphones, and I could hear it scratching out and his arm was up drumming on the window and blocking my view. Across the way were the small children who made a lot of noise and fought at each other so that they were always shooking and twisting in their seats, begging for some attention. I woke up and thought I was in the wrong place, and then when I remembered that I had taken a seat on this train to come home again, I did not feel happy. I had a great desire for the lavatory. This is usual for me, after sleeping. On the coach I never slept, unless I knew when there would be a stop.

On a train, of course, there are no stops. The lavatory is not just for cases of a particular and unstoppable emergency. I went, and it could have been worse. When I came back to my seat, the boy was reading a vividly-coloured magazine. The cover was the same red as my suitcase. 'That is the same colour as my suitcase,' I said to him. He did not look up. 'My suitcase is red like your magazine,' I repeated, and I rapped his magazine, so he knew what it was that I was talking about.

'Eh?'

'I have a red suitcase.'

'Wassat?'

'I want to look out the window. Please be so good as to move your arm down.' He did not move his arm. I did not like him.

The children across the way were pulling at each other's hair. I could not distinguish if they were boy children or girl children, but I do remember that they both had grubby locks down to their shoulders, and they were both exceptionally ill favoured. I decided that their parents must be in the seat in front of them, because no one else would love the children enough to put up with the back of their seat being pummelled so continuously without some form of admonishment. 'It is a long journey, and your children move a lot.' They looked round, but they didn't seem to see me. I tried addressing the children directly. 'Stop moving. You annoy me.' They stopped still and looked at me. One of them was wearing a red jumper. I leant across to get a better look. 'I like your jumper.' Then the parents were able to see me, suddenly. The man put an arm out, and pushed me back into my seat, not gently, and the woman said it was a shame and shouldn't be allowed. I completely agreed with her. The children started to pinch and writhe again, and I opened my mouth to tell them to stop again, but the man was watching me and not smiling, and nothing came out of my mouth. It was as if his silence was sucking away my words, leaving me with no air in my chest.

It hurt, having no air in my chest. I tried to cough, and I couldn't. Then the air came back all of a sudden and took me by surprise, and I must have not made a noise out loud because the man huffed and turned back around, away from looking at me. After that I sat still and concentrated on breathing for a while, and listened to the towns pass by with the train announcements. Although I wasn't in the mood for reading yet, the edges of my book cut into my palms in a very pleasing way as I held it tightly.

The train was very hot. My bladder was pressing on my attention again. I followed nature's call along to the toilet. It was occupied, and I had to wait in the ricketing hallway until a bone-thin lady emerged. She looked right through me. Perhaps I had annoyed her by knocking on the door and asking how long she would be, perhaps she didn't want to be associated with matters of the digestive system. The toilet did not smell as bad as the last time I had used it, although perhaps I had simply adjusted to the indignity.

This is where it all begins. This is the leaping point, the tipping point, the breaking point. I was in the toilet, so I didn't see the story start. Neither did I suspect that it might. I finished up my business, and I did up my belt, and I washed my hands as best as possible in the tiny sink. I didn't want to fall over in the train toilet, and the train rocked as it sang along, but I didn't want to touch the walls to steady myself either. Then I came out, back out into the hallway, and found that there was a fat lady waiting to push past me, rude as anything, huffing her cheeks out and scowling as if I had been in there playing cards to pass the time, simply to spite her. I stood and looked out the window for a moment, I'm sure it wasn't more than a moment. If I had gone back to my seat at that precise moment in time, perhaps the story would not have started. Everything is a perhaps. Nothing is certain in this life except death, and who knows, maybe not even death. I don't know yet.

There was a man in my seat. Not a young man, not an old man. In his forties, if I was forced to guess. He was sitting next to the boy with his headphones on and his black clothes and his glum way of looking out into nothing. He was sitting across from the scrabbling, mewling children. He was definitely sitting in my seat, holding my book half-open in his lap. 'You're sitting in my seat' I said, keeping my voice low so as not to disturb anyone else. He looked up at me in an interested way, and smiled.

'Can I help you?'

'That's my seat that you're sitting in.'

'I'm afraid you must be mistaken. This is my seat.'

'My seat.' I echoed plaintively, but he simply shook his head slowly, put my book down on the fold-out table in front of him, reached out, took my hand, and patted it gently. I repeated myself. He repeated his consolatory gesture.

'Do you have your reservation?' I did not. I did not recall having made one. I also did not have my wallet. That's when I realised that he was wearing my jacket. I pointed this out and he frowned, let go of my hand and pulled the top of his chest back like an affronted pigeon. He put his hand down on top of my book, and stroked it with his fingertips, as if it were a cat. The fat lady came huffing back along the aisle at this point, and tried to get past me. Then everybody joined in on the act, telling me to sit down, telling me I was making a nuisance. Nobody wanted to know about the man taking my seat and my jacket.

I sat in a spare table seat further along the carriage, joining a silent Chinese family who looked at me as if I was about to eat them. I explained about my jacket, but they stayed silent. I don't think they can have understood me. I was completely awake, and feeling bunched in on myself with worry. The train was a metal monster, and I was digesting in its stomach. I looked up the rows of seats and down back along the row again, in case there had been a mistake, but there wasn't.

I got up again. 'Give me back my jacket or I will call the police.' The threat had no effect, even though I was speaking almost loudly. He blinked at me and then sighed. I changed tack, raising my voice further and speaking over him at the boy in the headphones. 'Tell him. Tell him this is my seat. Tell him I've been sitting here, next to you.' The boy looked at me, looked at the man, then looked out the window with renewed glumness and a complete lack of interest in my predicament. I turned to the parents of the annoying children. 'You remember me?' It seemed he chose not to. 'You spoke to me, less than an hour ago.' He was not willing to either acknowledge or repeat the experience.

There was something quintessentially British about it. Everyone expressed their sense of community by sitting with their hands folded on their lap, eye contact slipping off to one side, and mouths pressed firmly shut. If it had been the Continent, there would have been a battle of shouting. If my wife had been there, she would have had her finger pushed into the interloper's chest, she would have challenged him at the top of her voice, and railed at the other passengers and then at the heavens until one of them answered her. Sometimes I miss my wife. But this was not a Spanish train, and my Spanish wife has been gone for many years. Everyone in hearing distance was embarrassed for me, and I joined them in wishing the problem would apologise quietly, go away politely, and stay away respectfully.

I did not go away. I reached out my hand and I plucked at the sleeve of my very own jacket, needing to feel that it was substantial, that it was real. It felt rough and cool between my fingers, and the blue veins on the back of my hands throbbed. I was asked to let go. The train was very hot. I was asked again, and I realised that I was crying. The tears were shaming down my cheeks and I could hear a high, thin sound like a far away kettle. It was me. I was keening as much as crying. The flush of embarrassment was spreading through the carriage, and the hairs left on my body were prickling into an all over itch of shame. Everything felt wrong, from the fit of my skin to the way all those eyes were pretending not to look at me. I tried one more time, in a very small voice. 'Please give me back my jacket.' He told me to go away in a voice that was empty of sympathy. I went back to the table with the Chinese family. Their silence was welcoming. I wiped my tears away on my shirt sleeve. The little boy was sitting very still, very quiet. Applying great care and attention, he was colouring in a picture of a dinosaur with a red crayon. The train pulled into another station and I didn't catch the name of it. It was hard to listen to the announcer with so many thoughts flying through my head, and it was hard to keep from crying again. The background chatter grew back again, and that's how I knew for certain that everyone had stopped talking and had been staring at me. The train was hot, and I was almost glad not to have my jacket. It was made of wool; natural fibres are the best for keeping the heat in this inclement climate of ours.

The dinosaur was a long necked one with a small head and ridges along its back. The small Chinese boy had done a very good job of colouring the ground beneath it green and the sky above it blue, although the tree off to one side was a very scruffy piece of work in brown. He was using a proper wax crayon, and pushing down hard to make the red of the dinosaur's body as dense and rich a colour as could be achieved. I watched the tip of the crayon flatten into the paper and felt like I was forgetting something important.

From all the sniffing and the tears, my nose felt as bad as if I had a heavy cold. I reached into my jacket pocket for a handkerchief and my hand went down into the plastic ridge of the seat beside me. The Chinese woman shifted herself closer to the window to give me greater flailing room. No more jacket, no more handkerchief. But I was rich in memory, and I had a home to go to. I must have had a home to go to, because I remember that I was going home. Home is where the heart is. Or where the hearth is. Burning love, either way. Warming, melting, helping love. Scalding, scolding, raking love. Red hot love. Red hot. Red. Red like the crayon. Red like my suitcase.

The train shuddered and stopped; we were at a station. I stood up and saw the man wearing my jacket stand up like a puppet, connected to me with invisible strings. I put my hand up to point at him but another passenger got in my view of him, then another one knocked me as they pulled their possessions down from the luggage rack. The rudeness of people hurts me deeply, and I opened my mouth to bellow like a bull against the injustice, but all that came out was a hot puff of air because, through the window, I saw the man in my jacket slipping away in the crowd with a bright flash of red thumping along his side, clutched in his scheming, thieving, dirty hand.

There was no time to stop and mull over what to do. I joined in the pushing and the shoving and I made it off the train. When I reached the platform, I saw the flash of red running round a corner and I ran after it.

Ahead of the crowd, I reached the ticket barrier and I lost that man. The barrier wouldn't give, and I bruised my hip trying. 'Give us your ticket,' said a man in uniform. 'I'll help you with that.' I explained the man in front had taken my bag. He asked for my ticket again. The thief, he had it all. Dignity, most of all. It took begging to be let through. Waverley Station was full of people running. None of them had my red suitcase. I stood and wept.

When I had run out of tears, I tried to go back to the train. From the wrong side of the barrier, I watched it leave. I went back to the main circle of the station, and tried to find a policeman. There was no luck there.

However, I did find a place called the Left Luggage. 'My luggage has left,' I said, by way of explaining why I was troubling them. 'In the possession of the wrong person.' They laughed. One of them gave me a seat for a bit, then walked me across to the Lost Luggage desk.

'A man took my things and then he was cruel to me beyond human reason,' I said, and the girl behind the desk sighed and tipped her head to one side. We were getting on uncommonly well, until she asked where my train was going. 'Home,' I said. She straightened her head up, and asked me again for no reason at all. I tried to say more about it, but the words didn't match up to my thoughts. She gave me a handful of forms and told me to fill them out. I asked her for directions to the toilet and left the desk.

There was a cleaner and his things round the corner from the toilets, mopping up something pink. He told me it was milkshake. We lamented the decline in modern manners. He asked where I was headed to, and I admitted that there might be some uncertainty over that.

'What town, chief?'

'Just home.'

'Nah, what station is that then?' I couldn't say. There was a temporary dislike between us. I broke it by showing him my forms. He asked if I could write and just right then, I felt that perhaps I couldn't. So he leant his mop up against the tiles and said he'd give me a head start. 'Surname?' I shook my head. 'First name? What do they call you?' I looked at the pink puddle near my feet. It had smears in it. 'You taking the piss, chief?' I walked away. He tried to give me the forms back, and I shook him off.

Back at the Lost Luggage desk, the girl was on the telephone. I stood in front of her until she looked at me, balanced the phone under her chin, and addressed me directly. 'Hi, yeah? Have you finished filling out them forms, yeah?' I held up my empty hands. She spoke into the phone. 'Got to go, yeah? Someone's here, right?' and hung up.

'I want my suitcase, please. And my jacket. And my book. Everything else is in either the jacket or the suitcase. It should all still be in order. Please.' She shook her head and gave a small shrug.

'No red suitcases handed in, yeah? Got those forms?' I explained that I had lost the forms. She commented that I would probably forget my own name next. I agreed that I had. She also asked if I thought I was being funny. I shook my head.

With nothing more but another handful of forms and a sense of being unwelcome, I walked back towards the toilets. They had the same barriers as the train platform. They cost a scandalous thirty pence.

There was nothing in my pockets. I spotted the cleaner coming out of a cupboard and went to sit on a bench by the ticket machine with my back to him. The bench was cold through my trousers, and I thought that if I was at home, wherever my home was, I would probably be having a cup of tea and a piece of toast about now. I tried to picture my hair and couldn't think of anything except the bench I was sitting on. I tried to picture taking the bread out of wherever I kept it. Nothing came, no image of a fridge or a cupboard or a pantry. No key in the lock, no front door.

Finally, I saw a policeman. I walked up and asked him for the time. He pointed out the electronic screen above our head. I thanked him and walked away.

I asked a girl buying a ticket who I was and she grabbed at her change from the machine, dropping half of it on the floor. I bent over to help her pick it up, not particularly quickly with my knees the way they are, and she put her shoe over the coins nearest me.

I sat back down and looked at the forms again. They made no sense; I couldn't answer any of the questions. I looked up, and the policeman was looking at me. He wasn't smiling.

I needed fresh air. I followed the signs for the way out, and there it was—a great grey ramp with taxis coming down, and people walking up one wide pavement on the side. Edinburgh is all about the hills, that much I knew, even then. Hills and narrow passages. Hidden turnings and countless steps. Such a pleasure to find a ramp, so much easier on the knees.

The forms were as useful to me as pigeon feathers. I stepped along the grey ramp up into the outside world, letting them fall from my hand as I walked.

It was so cold. I lost hold of my breath and had to knock my chest with my fist and cough to keep breathing. It was almost dark, a half-lit greyness stretched across the sky above the city buildings. I had not expected such coldness. It struck me for the first time, very deeply, that I really was without the protective layer of my jacket.

Stepping off the train had started a process where the world I knew peeled away, revealing a most monstrous core. There I was, as good as naked and exposed to the elements. I tried to explain this to a man who walked up next to me. He upped his pace and left me. 'I'm naked,' I said to two women. They looked me up and down, then turned and went back the direction they had come from. I looked after them and saw that they had stopped to talk to some policemen in yellow jackets. It was rude of them not to talk to me.

I tried to go back down into the station, but ended up in a glass-lined shopping centre. It was brightly lit, and the further I walked into it the warmer I got. The people around me walked slowly and smiled, and I knew it was a better choice. Even still, as I walked past the brightly coloured shop fronts, it felt like the mannequins turned their heads to watch me whenever I looked away from them. One of them waved.

Once I had made a full track round the top layer of the shopping centre, I felt tired. There was nowhere to sit down. I found a moving escalator and rode down to the next level. The shop mannequins started whispering cruel slander. I rode back up, but it seemed even colder this time.

I walked round and rode down and walked round and rode down until I did not know which way was the sky. After forever, I reached the bottom and knew I had gone to heaven. There were seats all around me, and I could smell food. There was a free public toilet.

Once I was sitting down on a table by myself and I was quiet, I could feel my heart settling in my chest. The table was formed from smooth plastic and it was clean. Then someone walked by me, and I watched them go, and saw that the automatic doors back outside were close to hand.

I moved, because of the draft.

Although the new table was not clean, I did not mind. I ate the rest of the burger, then put the empty carton in the rubbish bin. It felt so good to help out, I did the same on the next table along. Moving slowly, nobody really watched me.

I had not realised how hungry I was or just how late it must have been until I had that first bite. Eating only made me hungrier. I cleared all the tables in a guilty shuffle that took me deeper and deeper into the food court. Away from the shop windows I was invisible.

The family at the table next to me started putting babies in buggies and messing around with rucksacks. The eldest child stared straight at me, scowling. I stuck my tongue out at him. He put down his Coke and stood up. I looked at my knees. There was a stain on my trousers, so I picked at it.

When the family had gone, I went and sat in the boy's seat. I took his straw out and drank his Coke. The ice in it had not finished melting. I had wanted something hot—even in the heart of the place, it was not as warm as I would have liked, without my jacket.

With sugar in my veins, I started on the doughnuts. Such unhealthy eating habits for young children. I was glad for their own sake they had not finished the tray.

The bubbles of the Coke scraped at the inside of my throat. Perhaps I drank it too fast. I was so thirsty. So hungry, so thirsty, so tired. It is true that there is no place like home. I began to wish I had never left my home. Whatever desire had driven me out was lost as everything else.

After the doughnuts I did not want to eat any more. Satiated, something stirred in my heart and I stood up and set off home, trusting to muscle memory. I took two steps and then the surging feeling of hope passed and I was stranded again.

Without physical or mental direction, I decided to ask for help. People seemed to be leaving at a rate, and pickings were slim. There was a couple not too far away. They were about my age, and I was sure they would be able to point me in the right direction.

They were also getting ready to leave. The woman was taking their tray over to the bin, balancing her handbag in the crook of her arm and moving in small bird jerks. I could not see any food left on the tray. I went across to their table slowly, trying to think of the right words to say. I had to move chairs out of my way, and I started feeling scared for no reason at all. I did not think that I had ever felt like that before, but I was finding it increasingly hard to remember how anything ever was.

Then, before I reached them, she fell over. There must have been some wrappings on the floor, or a loose tile. Perhaps she did not have good balance. She wailed a little as she fell. Her man left fussing over their things and went straight to help her. He left their shopping bags so quickly that one fell over on its side. She was lucky to be looked out for like that. Other people came too, and I found myself next to her, picking up her handbag from where she had dropped it and holding it out to her husband.

Her husband waved his hand towards the rest of their things. Perhaps he said something, told me to put it down. I am sure he thanked me. They were good people, with manners and happiness. It is easy to tell. They were clearing their table, for example.

Perhaps that is why I did what I did. Everyone was round the woman in a circle, and I remember that there was talk of an ambulance and so forth. But I was not worried about her; I expect she just broke her hip, or bruised herself rather than something serious.

When you are old, you expect to die. They were older than I was. I remember that now. Old like I was, but older than I was.

I put the handbag down with the plastic bags of all the things they had been accumulating. The husband's coat was lying on the seat of a chair. I put down the handbag and I picked the coat up. Thick wool, black. Proper lining. Afterwards, I regretted that I had not kept hold of the handbag. My priority then was getting my jacket back, I had not thought about needing a handbag as well. It is easy to live with regrets. I walked away with the coat over my arm. It was too heavy to hold like that comfortably, especially walking as fast as I did.

I was going up in the world via the moving escalator before I looked back. The old woman was sitting up on the floor and her husband's arm was around her. They looked perfectly fine. I raised my free arm to wave. I did not wave; they were not looking at me. I put my hand on the moving escalator rail to steady myself. At the top I put the coat on; it was a perfect fit, and smelt of pipe tobacco, which was comforting.

My aunt—I think my aunt but perhaps a grandmother or a family friend—smoked pipes. Wearing this coat was to be folded in her arms while the puppies play at her feet. She wears a man's hunting jacket and the wax on it leaves dark smears on my leg. We visit her every Mayday and I learn about the mechanics of breeding cattle and gorge on early blackberries. One year we stop going and she is never mentioned again and I only remember her through smelling other people. But I didn't remember this on the escalator, I only sensed a subtle reassurance.

I kept going up, and went out the way I came in. Walking back through the upper levels of the shopping centre, all the shutters were coming down and blocking in the mannequins. Everyone else was carrying plastic bags and talking loudly. They all looked tired. I remembered how to retrace my steps.

There was an awareness in me that this was somewhere I could neither stay nor return to. At that point, it did not sink in quite that I might want to come back somewhere which was warm and had free food and free toilets. I did not know how lucky I was. Perhaps I had been lucky before in my life; I did not remember. All my memories were there until I tried to look directly at them. But I could feel them inside me, floating.

If I had not taken the coat then perhaps I would have been able to return. The story would have twisted in a different way and perhaps I would have been brought to a different ending. I developed mixed feelings about that, later. But at that time, I was outside in the fresh air and I was warm in this very smart coat, and it felt acceptable.

The world was a beautiful carnival. The darkness was full, with stars up high suggesting frost later on. In front of me was a Ferris wheel of considerable size, flashing in patterns and colours. The trees were strung with small ice-blue lights; I had walked into a fairytale.

I lost myself in a town of small, overtly Teutonic wooden stalls. There were so many people around that anyone trying to hunt down me or my new coat would have to have given up straight away. There were free sample plates of strudel and Stollen. I put some in my coat pockets. I walked into this magical, open-air counterpart to the food court I had just left, where the air smelt of hot wine and apple-spices. Families and young couples fingered the candles and decorations on the stalls. Some of them ate Würst in buns. I stood and watched them.

Princes Street was as busy as if it were daytime. Out here, the shop shutters stayed up. I looked at the entrance to Jenners and let my mind run away with itself; I was twenty again and buying gloves for my best girl. They cost a week's wage. They were bright red. Harlot gloves. Soft leather. She was next to me, laughing and trying on pair after pair. Her hands were so small, most of them just fell off her.

I crossed the road and went in. The doors were heavy to push open, but a stranger helped. He looked at my coat and he smiled and said something but I pushed past him.

Everything was different. So busy. The ceiling was strung with baubles, and the counters were full of cosmetics. It was bright, but softly so. It was warm. The floor was wet with all the customers coming in and out. I walked through to the back hall, and stared up.

The Christmas tree was ridiculously large. I laughed. The fairy trees from outside were following me. Or I had shrunk. If I had shrunk, so had everyone else, so it did not seem particularly important. I looked at the tree and I laughed. 'It isn't real,' said a woman next to me. 'They switched to artificial last year.' I looked at her, and she nodded as if very satisfied.

'I'm looking for gloves,' I said. 'For my fiancée.' She told me to try the basement. We stood next to each other and looked at the tree for a while.

It was truly a pleasure to stroll around the department store. It was not as I remembered it, but I misplaced myself in the present and touched silk scarves, stroked fur, and smelt all the perfumes in the Lady departments. Lots of shop assistants helped me search for the perfect gift.

'It's for my wife,' I explained to each of them in turn. 'It has to be very special.' They made cooing noises and told me about the bespoke gift wrap service, which sounded very reasonably priced, considering they used real satin ribbons. If I had spent over a hundred and fifty pounds then the wrapping would have been free.

The furniture department was thankfully quiet. I found the most comfortable of the armchairs and had a little nap. When I woke up my neck was stiff, and I considered moving along to see if they also stocked mattresses. But there was a shop boy trying to help me most adamantly, so I didn't.

Once I had explained that my son was in Silverware and would be back soon to collect me, he left me alone. It was most restful there, and I was touched by the dedication to customer care that I experienced. Everyone kept asking me if I was quite alright. I felt like a new puppy.

If it had not been for the security guard, I would have been quite content to live in that consumer paradise for as long as happily ever after. I did not make it up to the food department, but I am certain that it far outshone either the one in the shopping centre or the stalls outside.

Back out on the street, I waved at the security guard to show I was sorry for the words I had spoken in haste. My shoulder was sore, but I forgave him the misunderstanding. In his position, perhaps I would have reacted the same way. I have not always been economical with my fists myself. He pulled the shutters down then most of the lights went off. The other stores were doing the same, and would not let me in.

Still being half asleep, I walked back to the doors of the shopping centre before I remembered that I was not supposed to be there, just in case. They were locked anyway. The Ferris wheel cranked round, and my neck felt cold. The sounds of the funfair began to leech of appeal. I walked into a bar. Old, ornate, grand. Café Royal. I sat at a booth and watched the other patrons come in and out. It was a lovely place to come to with a group of friends, I could see that much. There was no loose change in the pockets of my new coat, nothing in my trousers. I ate the cake samples from the wooden huts. There was a sticky patch inside one pocket where I had leant on the marzipan during my nap.

My poor, poor cherry red suitcase. I wondered where you were. I wondered where the rest of me was. Poor, poor me. I missed the company of my book most particularly. The night before, in the room without a television or even a radio, I had read five chapters before falling asleep on top of the counterpane. Half the memory slipped in and out of my grasp, like a fish. I could feel my fingers flicking through the book, smoothing down the pages with the flat of my hand, picking at the curling cellophane cover. The name of the B & B flickered in the background and when I tried to focus on it then it swam away and was lost in the watery eddies swirling in my head. My book was nothing more than a half-forgotten dream, but sitting in the bar felt barely more real. There was a pile of free papers stacked up on a stand and they passed the time with me, but it wasn't the same. Newspapers are so flimsy. I thought about vinegar and grease soaking through them. People in the booth next to me ordered food.

Once I finished reading the paper, I read it backwards. Then chose pages at random. The time went somewhere else. The bar filled up. Nobody asked to sit in my booth. The staff left me alone and I was quiet and still.

Trying to remember where I wanted to go next, I remembered that thieving bastard on the train. My suitcase, gone. My jacket, gone. There was something which itched at me, inside my head.

'Is there something here? Something just here on my scalp?' I asked the couple nearest my booth. They looked at me and saw reassurance in the expensive cloth of my coat, and leant in. The girl shook her head, spilling her wine slightly.

'Does it hurt?' the man asked. I told him it did not. I explained it was itching. They leant backwards. The man coughed something, and they went to the bar.

There were more books in my suitcase, I was certain of that. Books in my suitcase waiting to be read. A book in my hands, tipping on my lap when I slept on the train. A book left on my seat when I stood up and walked out of myself.

Where had the book been when I came back? Turning over and over in that man's hands. Long fingers flicking idly through my pages. Dirty thief taking the words out of my mouth.

'Are these seats free. Excuse me? Hello?' A pair of businessmen, their suits shiny from wear. They muscled in on my space, and their slopping pints of lager left large wet rings on my newspaper, for which they apologised curtly. I listened to them talking about their secretary's legs. One of them had a book in his pocket. 'Is that my book?' I asked them. They didn't seem to understand. I reached out and took it.

The business men were not in the mood for sharing their book with me. I didn't recognise the cover, but there are different editions. Different jackets on the same text, disguising, hiding. Hiding my book from me. Now, now I knew what had happened. This was when I realised the secret. This is when I knew what conspiracy had been levelled against me. It wasn't the first time. They've been after me all my life. They stole my son, they stole my wife. Now it seems they thought they could steal me. But I was on to them; at last I had their number.

The barmen at the Café Royal were very strong. It only took two of them to lift me into the street.

All the warmth of my anger stayed with me as I ran along the road and back to the train station. There were buses getting in my way, and shouting all behind me, but I just ran on. Finally I was at the gates of Waverley Station in all vengeance, and they were locked against me. The cowards. Thought they could keep me out with their metal bars.

They could.

Locked out of my life, I needed back in that station for a good reason; I had to get my book back. It was all so clear. That man took my book. I was only halfway through. Halfway through a book, of course I was confused. The point only becomes clear at the end. He took away everything I'd worked so hard to learn. I needed my book back, and then I could read it to the end. Then I'd know who I was, and where I was meant to be. I had lost the plot and I needed the book to show me how the pieces fitted back together in a way that made sense.

The book was with the man, or on the train. I wanted it back. I wanted to be myself again. It was time to be home.

The bars were as thick as my wrist. My arms were too tired to pull me up them; they've been too tired for antics like that for several years. I hit them instead. There was no pain, the cold took it away. The cold took everything away. I was seeping out into the night, hanging in front of my mouth like my visible breath. Oh, and it was terrible.

That night was not my finest. I found a stairwell, up on the hill that reaches the Royal Mile. There was too much tiredness in my bones to go any further. I huddled in my new coat and I put the newspaper underneath me and I waited for the night to pass.

Covered in a glittering frost, with the fairy lights of the trees in the distance and a stillness of no wind, it was breathtaking. I turned my collar up. Sleep happened, of a sorts.

When the object hit me, I did not know where I was. The wetness across my knees, and the smell of beer told me it had been a can. The coat cushioned most of the blow. I felt every joint in my body as a small, dull pain, and knew a new level of coldness.

The group was standing not so far away, below me on the stairs. They jeered. They drew closer. They taunted me. Eventually they left. Then, shortly afterwards, a lone figure came running back up. A man, by the height of him. I sat and waited. He tossed a packet into my lap. He left.

The chips were cold, and half of them gone from the polythene tray inside the wrappings. I almost missed the note; it had ketchup on it. Twenty pounds. People act according to their conscience, it seems. Or perhaps I was being paid for my entertainment. I licked it clean. I expect he was the one who kicked my neck. I will never know for certain.

The dawn came with a greyness of heavy clouds that I knew in every aching tendon meant snow. My hands were mottled purple as I held them in front of my face; during my sleep, they had slipped from my pockets. There was new frost on the chip wrappings on my lap. I rubbed the tears from my cheeks and found blood smeared round my ear. I took my time in standing up, then hit my chest to cough out the lumps in my throat.

Most pressing was my need to use some facilities. There was nobody around as I pissed against the step I had slept on. Even if there had been a crowd, I could not have done anything else. I would have done it in my mother's parlour.

My ears rang as I went down, back to Waverley Station. The gates were unlocked, but I couldn't remember why I had cared so much. I walked down the ramp and sat on a bench, watching the cleaners pick the rubbish from between the racks with their long mechanical arms. The Lost Property Office was still closed.

Once the concession stands began opening, I broke the twenty pound note buying a cup of hot tea. The girl gave me a funny smile, and a bag of cookies. She asked me something but I couldn't hear her properly; the ringing had moved into a roaring, like water in a tunnel.

That night, I found somewhere better to sleep. It was occupied, but I persuaded the tramp to move. I wiped the blood off my shoes with one of the blankets he left behind, and slept with his smell at the back of my throat.

There were new staff at the Lost Property Office almost every day. I used their forms to wipe my arse. Beggars can be choosers.

Write or Die

- Sandra Jensen -

I done him no wrong. None that no one else would in a sharp night under the prickle trees. A black heart he had and teeth brown as a fethered bat dropped in shit. Cow shit to be exat. That cows got a name and her names Petal. But no one knows this around here they all think she cant hear nothin but she can. She cleverern most and then some. Thats not what Im here to tell you. Im here to tell you about the man with the black heart. I aint sayin it was black coloured in effect and now Im thinkin you might consider me racist or somethin but thats not what I mean neither. I mean he was evil. As evil as they come. He come and dug out my cows eyes jes for the fun of it.

I come upon him sleepin with a white rock underneath him naked as the day. Him, not the rock. Rocks tend to be naked most times. Some rocks like to spread themselves with moose mulch and the like and then Im thinkin thats not what I mean. I mean moss. Jes couldnt find the name so I made somethin up. I do that a lot.

Now your thinkin I made up the story about Bob Dunn. Bobs the one with the bad heart I done kill. Im stallin now, lost for words. This shit fessin is takin its time. You think I shuld stop? I bet you do. You get to think your thoughts and I get to think mine. Its a free world out there and its freer inside when a mans got time on his hands. Time to sit out on

23

a rick and friz his balls off. Thats what Im doin and I dont care who knows it. I dont mean rick I mean rock. It was my rock and that damn Bob lay down upon it as if it were a woman. I seen some crazy situations in my life but not that. Horses and the like. Cows too but not mine. I hate to think Bob took a shine to Petal. Petal deserved better. She deserved a soft bed and a good feed now and then. Come to think Im pretty hungry too but I aint seein much chance a feedin right about now. Its time for bed but I got one fekkin minute left the men with guns tell me. Time for my last croak Id say. No one in his right mind would a let me out a the cage Im in. Take the key away and throw it in the Oakey river would do me a kindness. I had a bad day. You think you had a bad day? Well think again. You dont know bad. It started with my mornin porridge cold and lumpy and then I burned it blackern a sooty sky. Then some bucktoothed fella name a Cody knocks on the door to tell me about Bob and the rock. Thats jes for starters. I went out to feed Petal and that about topped it off and made me know it was not goin to be a good day. No sir.

They tells me I got two choices. Write or die. Im not so dumb as I dont know which ones the better choice. I choose write but they dont know I dont write so god. God ha ha. Hes played no part in this game thats for sure. I gave up on that fella a long time ago. Im supposed to be tellin my fessin but its not so easy under these circumstances. They put a gun to my head. You try writin in them circumstances. OK OK, so Im stallin again but heck wouldnt you? I got ten minutes a time they says. Then they tells me to stop and they each goes out for a piss or somethin. Now they stickin it to me and shovin me here this Smith Corona machine. How anyone expects to writin a fessin in this situation I dont know. I like the name a this contraption howevers. Reminds me that TV show Alias Smith and Jones. Too bad about the fella that died. Guess we all gotta go.

Anyways the men that keep me here says Im screwin with the facts. They dont know the facts. No man does. Its between me and my maker and the owlish sky that lay over my friz body that fekkin prickle night. He left me hurtin. That Bob Gunn fella who my vr good friend Ruthie calls Bob Dung. Shed be about right about that. He a shitty smellin man if ever there was one and Ive reason to know. You ask me if he did that to the cow. Well he did. Im not lyin about them eyes. He considered Petal a witness to his felony and she was. He be not too bright so I suppose I should credit him for thinkin maybe Petal got powers more than most but she dont not really. She hears and she sees but she dont speak at least not to me. Not more than a moo or two like any normal cow.

OK so I got to fess the whole story but I dont see what good that does me. I can tell you Bobs meaner parts but not the hole damn thing. Hes well hes shit. I mean a shit. Hes my family yes and I knows you not supposed to say bad words about your family but when a mans been treated like a fekkin asshole then a mans got a right to say whatever he likes about nother. Now they pokin me with that dam firearm again. I dont like to be pressured. Told what I knew. Not all of it but whatever I got winter for. Shit. Winter dont figure in my fessin not less you mean when hell frizes over. What I mean is witnesses. I told you I dont right too good. So yes sir I got witnesses for Petals vandalism but not the rock intimicy and the rest. Im not so stupid I dont know how the law works. You need someone else to factor in your lies or your truth tellin and your truth tellin needs, what they call it? Corroborashin? Thats what they call it.

I can describe the rock but I aint goin too far with that one because they prod the gun further up my belly jes to hurt me more. They dont know what real hurtin is. They think a poke in the belly is bad. Well let me tell you I been poked far worse places by that dung fella Bob. He the kind thatll poke anythin that he can fit in. And hes a bigun lemme tell you. That poor disturbed rock had a hole innit where rats curled. Now Bob dont know this which is the reason bein he rose up outa it like he done shoved his pecker in a hot potato. I dont see this but I heard it. Fair raked out to me here over in the house not a hunnerd feet away.

Im a doin nother ten minutes even though them with the guns are asleep. I been considerin maybe its good for me to spell out my life. My friend Ruthie says I got notions to tell people and if I keep them bottled up all this time Im gonna explode. I get to thinkin that maybe shes right. Things on my mind that dont credit no one. Situations Ive seen and Ive known that are makin me bloat up like a sheep with that puffin sickness. Whats goin to happen to me if I bloat fattern big Alice the bull over in the McTabbarts place? I aint sayin. I havnt done this much writin before so Id not know what happens to someone like me.

Id better start at the beginnin. I said he were family. That was no lie. But theres other family that done me wrong. Bob aint the first. Hes my Paws brother. They say blood runs thicker in family. I dont have no brother so I dont know about that. I had a sister once but shes dead. Died newborn. I dint even get to see her. Neither did my Ma. Shes dead too. Clean gone. My sisters also a killer I guess you could say. Maybe killin runs in the family. I guess it must do since my Paw done kill so many livin things I loss count. But no man. My paws not a man killer not that I knows of. Maybe hes a woman killer if you considers puttin Ma in the family way with my sister killin her. Maybe havin to sleep with him was bad enough. Id a thought so. Least he aint done that with me. No sleepin. Fek no. Udder things but no sleepin. Anyways I don know where my Paw be these days. He went off after that and he leave me alone. Good riddance Ruthie says. She call him Vernon the turd. Ruthy got a worsun dirty mouth than me. So I think maybe I got some reason to do a man wrong.

Im gettin lost now. I think maybe theres some reason in the perticular times my ten minutes of writin happen. Maybe I need that firearm up my ass to make me speak the truth. But I am spinnin the truth. Fek I don mean that, I mean speakin the truth. I never lie. As I ready said I sometimes make things up but thats not the same as lyin. I was tellin you about. What? Shit I aint rememberin anythin anymore. I got me a headache thatll kill a stoat. I jes want to go to sleep now, but I aint sleepin cause a the howlin outside. This place got wolves and other animals. Less these days since my Paw kill most of em. He liked his gun. But not so much he dint leave one for me. Jes one mind, he took the shotgun his grandpaw gave him. I wanted that one but he dun give me the udder one. It worked good on Bob Dung so I guess I shouldnt be complainin none.

Im not doin so well. Im slowin down. I think I need to eat somethin but they only give me water. I guess thats somethin. And a hard bed. Im wonderin if they buried my cow. She dint live after that eye gougin. Who coulda? I did right by her I did. What kinda man does that do a poor animal? A man not right in the head. Thats what me an Ruthie think. She spotted it earlier but thats cause Bobs her Paw.

Im still down here and they aint disturbed me with a gun or nothin. Im wonderin if they gone and left me. I drunk up all my water. I dint know they might leave me with nothin more. I was writin my last bit a fessin in the night and I heard some rumblin and a crash and I thinks maybe they beatin up on some udders. I dont know for sure if there are any more than me but I thinks so. But what I thinks dont mean much. Anyways I were lyin on my hard bed all night after my writin session and I couldnt stop thinkin. It was like my brain got nuts and bolts on it movin fastern a water wheel in the Oakey river that runs so fekkin quick I lost my boat once. Thats nother story you dont need hear about. I was considerin you might think since Bob Dunn was Ruthies Paw that makes Ruthie a Dung too. But it dont. This fessin business is complicated.

Ruthies Ma has nother man. The fella everone thinks is Ruthies Paw. Hes OK I suppose his names dishpan hand Hank. Thats one a Ruthies names. He got hands biggern a cow pat. He uses em too. He dont know Ruthies not his. Everone else knows but not him and he better not find out. So Im considerin maybe I carry on with this fessin and cover all the details of my lie. LIFE. I dont mean lie. Damit. I don lie.

So I was tellin you. I came upon Bob on the rock. Well that runnabout fella with the buckteeth name a Cody who digs in his field at wird times come to the door to tell me about Bob on the rock but Id already heard Bobss unwholesome shouts as I said. Thats what made me go out with my Paws gun and find him out there under the sickly moon and some stars. I dont like the night much but I went anyways. The prickle trees were pricklin and I dint have my boots on cause I dint want Bob to hear me nor the wolves or any other animal that my Paw might not ready killed. I found Bob on the rock nursin his poker and cryin out like a woman. I crept away cause I heard Petals wailin. It was a bad night lemme tell you. what with Bobs cryin and her wailin I thought I was gone be torn in two. I get back to the barn and thats when I found her. Blood everwhere. And then some. I was so mad but I couldnt leave Petal there like that. She werent dead. She were half there but not fulsome like. So I shot her. That pained me more than what I then went and did. I shot her good. One to the head straight on. I knows where to point my gun if I dont have to hold it too long. Its a heavy un. I waited till she stopped movin which took a while. You dont know what thats like. You think youve cuxassed more sufferin but its not the case. They dead but somethin other is movin in them for a while. Her hooves and legs movin like shes runnin over the back field with them little happy flowers, gallopin more like, gamblin I think they call it. When those hooves stopped their drummin I went out to find Bob on the rock. He wernt there. He probably heard the gunshot and scuttled into the woods. I dont like it in there but I went anyway. It was vr dark in there much darker than outside where I generally prefer it. I heard owls and scratchy things. The needles were pokin into my feet cause as I told you I dint have my boots on. I held that damn gun close but it was weighin down my hand somethin fierce. I knew I had to find him quickly or Id be a gonner. I prayed to God I find him quick.

I knows I said I dont believe in God no more and its true but that dont stop a man prayin. I never told you what Bob did to Ruthie and Im not goin to. My fessins only about me and my own doins. The men pokin me with the guns the ones who have gone and left me here in this cage in my own home said I wasnt to mention in any other facts than what I did and why. I tell them it were cause of Petal but they dont believe Id kill a man for that. Thing is I dont have my gun to prove it. I could show that the bullet in Petals head was the same as the one in Bobs but I lost that gun in them woods.

You might be wonderin how come I dint hear Petals wailin before I heard Bobs and why that Cody fella dint neither. Im a gettin to that but not yet.

I been down here a long time with no one lookin in on me. Not even a toothy rat or nothin. I think they done gone an left me to die. Id thought that Cody fella might come and check whats happenin but he dint. I jes got me and this damn contraption that tangles my fingers. I jes got my writin to do and thats bout it. I got nothin else. They dont left me any water or food but they left me a pile of this here paper. Maybe I aint playin my cards right. Maybe I shoulda told them about what I saw in the forest. That be worse then anythin. I was shivverin under a tree leg, tryin to warm myself against the bark. You know like bears and them things do. They rub themselves. Not for warmin for scritchin but if you rub it also warms you. I were tryin to do it quiet as I knew Bob was in there somewhere. Then I heard the cackle a leaves scrunchin. I nearly swallows my tongue.

It werent Bob. It were Ruthie. Now I dont know if I should be carryin on with this part of the fession as shes my vr good friend and I care for her more than most. I dont have many friends. Actually I dont have none but her. So I promises to protect her and I does. Im not tellin anythin. But I get to thinkin if Im left here to die then maybe it dont matter what I say. Otherwise I blow up. Ruthie herself said I have words to say and I should say them. But then I thinks if I do this writin business and then I die and then they come back they see what I write. I guess I can scrunch it up and eat it or somethin. Paper dont taste too good but jeez Im hungry. I could eat a horse. I dont mean what I say. I wouldnt eat horse if you paid me million bucks. Horses are creatures special like. They knows items about a man. They knows if they are good or just plain evil. My Paw could never ride without gettin himself thrown. As for Bob he got kicked so hard his shin busted in three. I saw the bones stickin out cause he dragged his self right here hopin for sympathy. I pretended I werent available. I shut my trap and dint move till Cody who were doin his wird diggin in the field past midnight heard Bob and then Cody come and shove Bobs pained body over his shoulder and takes him to the Doc. That Docs worsen Bob. I been once nvr again.

So I was tellin you about what happenin in the woods. I was clampin my mouth shut with one hand and my gun with the other. I dint want to scare Ruthie so I say nothin and I wondered what she was doin in them woods. Maybe she heard Bobs fekkin wailin or my poor Petal and then I wondered if Ruthie turned traitor on me and did that terrible activity to Petal. I only wondered for a short bit cause thats when Ruthie took out somethin long and gloomy from her coat. It was cold as I said so she wore her dad Hank with the dishpan hands coat. Hanks gone walkabout. He does that a lot. Anyways she took the object outa her coat and then I saw her point it in the general direction a somethin shifty in the burly bushes yonder. I were hopin she wernt up to what I thought she was up to but she were. Bob Dunns eyes gloamed like them cats eyes on a wavy road. I dint even have time to shut my ears. I thinks to myself that gun Ruthie points at him probably blows a wallop thatd deafen a bull. Even Alice the McTabbarts big bloated bull. Maybe specially Alice cause she one a them skittish types cause they dont treat her right. When the shotgun goes off it sound like a cannon in some vr bad war. It done kicked her back so hard she flew maybe a mans length behind herself which happend to be where I was standin iced with fright my own gun a yewsles object cause Id dropped it on my foot. I dint even cry out. I dint have to. Them fekkin gun did it for me cause it went off when it landed on my foot. It fires off some ways into them bushes too. But Im not wonderin about the bullets destination. I have got Ruthie to take care of. She been lyin there like shes been hit herself or somethin. I checked her body for bullet holes but I dont find none. She weepin a bit. Blood all down her legs. She got pretty legs. Much prettier than mine which is one reason I dont wear them fekkin skirts. Get in the way anyways. I asks her whats wrong and she says Bob did it. In the barn. With Petal lookin on. I dont need to asks what Bob did. He done it to me. Many times. Paw too. Sometimes together. Ruthie is lookin real bad and I dont knows what to do. I check the bushes for Bob but I dont hear nothin. Jes some creakin in the branches but I figger thats some night owl or nother bird that got woken with all them racket we made. Ruthies squirtin sounds like a kittens been stepped on. I hunch up close and tell her Im goin get her Ma considerin dish hands Hank gone walkabout. Mas dead, she says. Hank came back and used em hands on her again and once he quit sluggin he gone disappeared again. Fek I says.

The long and the short is Ruthie ran away case Hank came after her too like hes been known to. She thinks it be safe down in our barn with Petal. It werent. Bob there and I hate to think why. Maybe he doin that thing to Petal and when he sees Ruthie he thinks his luck is lookin up.

Im gettin me a sore hurtin in my hands peckin at this machine. My head hurtin too. I told you it were a bad night. Now I got more a this complicated fessin business to do. I guess Im gonna let it all out one ways or the others. Theres not been a sound from the men with guns and I figger Im goin to die down here so I might as well finish.

Ruthie there lyin on my foot and bleedin from her bottom hole. I dont know any other ways to say it Im sorry. I suspects she must a cracked her head when she fell cause thats bleedin too. I tell her dont talk but she says if she aint talkin now when will she. I dont have an answer to that so I shut up. She tells me Bob had a bottle of ass whup with him which the stupid fek left half empty when he goes lyin on my rock. But first he did that aberration to my cow. I dont want to repeat what Ruthie told about that business. You knows the situation. Anyways the whiskeys what quieted my Petal awhile. Ruthie gone crawled over to the poor beast and gives her a swig. I reckon Ruthie takes one too I mean who woudnt? I woulda. Then she sees the shotgun hidin under the water trough. Whats it doin there I dont know. I thought that gloomy object looked familiar. Jes like my granpaws and it were. I got thinkin that means my Paw come back and that dont give me a good feelin. On top a the no good feelin I already had so it were gettin pretty bad in there lemme tell you. Ruthie tells me once Petal quiet a bit she drags her bleedin self and the shotgun out the barn to find Bob and kill him.

Meanwhile Im hearin Bobs yells from em rats teethin his pecker and that Cody fella is at my door. I tell him to piss off. I guess he follows me cause next I hears him in the woods makin that crickle sound on the leaves again. Shit I says. Ruthie mumbles somethin. Probably shit too. I makes a grab for her shotgun but its so fekkin heavy I dont bother. I jes pretended I got it leveraged towards Cody. Its vr dark in there so when I tell him I got a gun eyein his pecker he believes me and comes out. He seems meek enough and tips his hat a bit. I notice he got it the wrong way round and I were about to say somethin to that effect but then I remember what Im about. So I point to the blackenin smidge a bushes that I think Bobs crushin and tell Cody to go check on the asshole. I got to do somethin with Ruthie so I strokes her hair. She says your not takin me to that fekkin creepball Doc and I say no I aint. She whispers a bit and I come close but theres some commotion in them bushes divertin my attention. Ruthie grabs my hand. I guess now I knows what a deth grip feels like. You put me in the Oaky river like that lady with the hair, she says. I know the lady she means cause she and I used a look at the picture together. Picture a vr pretty lady floatin dead down the river with her hair jes straggly bits a waterweed and her hands crossed all holy on her chest. Then Ruthies mouth closes and a bit of spit dribbles out the corner. She breathed her last and I was the one who heard it.

Codys draggin Bob. Bob dont look too good. Hes got a bullet hole right smack between his eyes size a fist. How the fek my handgun did that from a lyin position on my foot I dont know but it did. I knows the difference between a shotgun hole and a handgun hole and it werent Ruthie who killed him.

I tells Cody we got to put Ruthie in the river like she asks. Cody raises his wispy eyebrows and sticks out those teeth a his as if to make reasons why not but I dont let him. I tells him it were her last wishes so he shuts up and heaves her over his shoulder and I follow him to the river. Im glad a some company and the strong armin. Oakey river not far luckly jes the other sides the wood and maybe a piece or two. Cody lowers her ass gently as if she were one a them expensive cups my Ma said we were never to use. I dont understand why have a cup you never use but Ma wasnt the kinda woman you argue none with. I put some straggle weeds in Ruthies hands. Best I could do cause there wernt no flowers roundabout. I cross her hands over her chest like the picture and I strokes out her long hair so it floats same ways. Cody pushes her off and shes gone before I can say shit cause the river movin right along. I dont wanna see no one or speak neither. I nod my head at Cody and he gets the idea. Im gonna see to Bob he says an thats the last I sees a him.

I reckin its Cody told on me cause when I gets home and Im tryin to get some sleep the bangin on the door happens. Them men like a burnin forest shovin themselves at me an draggin my poor sorry self down here in the basement where I dont like it none neither. Jes me and this here typin machine to make my fessin. Ten minutes they gives me like I says. Ive been down here longern ten minutes thats for sure. I gone dried up words an all. Got nothin more to say. Im goin lie down now and never open my eyes again. I figger however deth is like it gotta be bettern what life served me up already. I dont ask for nothin but I sure got more than my fair share I reckon. Me an Ruthie too. She dont deserve to die like that. Me neither but I guess you dont have no say in how your life turns out. You jes gotta put one foot in front the other and hopes for the best. I aint exactly got the best but maybe someone else did. Maybe thats how it works. Maybe theres only so much good to go around so if you gets none someone else gets bit more. I feel better thinkin on that. Will thats it. Thats my fession and I hope it serves someone somewhere.

I guess I lied. But it aint a real lie cause I dint know I wernt goin to die. Told you I dont lie and I dont. I figgered I was goin to die for certain. I closed my eyes a good long while and waited. Deth sure takin its time I thinks. Then I hear a rattle I consider it my deth rattle but it aint and Im considerin its the men with guns again. Well I have my fessin all done so I aint movin or nothin. I jes lies there. I fair jump and let out a screetchin sound when I feel a mans hand on my head. He brush my hair gently as if he were my Ma only Ma never did that. It feel wird. Not too good actually. I dont like to be stroked the best a times. Aint had good experience with that stuff. Anyways its that wird fella Cody. We in the family way now but thats nother long story. He picks me up as if I were lighter than a peckin feather. He takes me to his house which is jes down the valley a bit. I dont struggle. I pretty weak with no water or food or nothin for days.

He tells me hes taken care a the men with guns and that they no lawmen they jes some friends of Bobs come do him justice and me some harm. He also took care a that dishpan hand Hank. And my Paw. And Bob. He done dug them into his field. Now I knows why he digs at wird times. He gotta few fellas in there he does. He tells me he been keepin watch over me and Ruthie ever since we been small. I laugh a bit when he tells me this cause Cody not much biggern me. Hes tall for a 17 yr old but not that tall. Hes 2 yrs older an me so we jes about right for one nother. Anyways he said he put anyones in there who been mean to us. Hes real nice to me and I says yes when he asks if I might think a marryin him. I aint never been taken care of like Cody takes care of me. He even put that hack Doc in his field when I told him what he did to me and Ruthie. We got a nice lady Doc now. She says Im doin well and all.

I been puttin some butterbeans and some potatoes and some pecker shape squash in Codys fields and they been growin jes fine. Especially the butterbeans and the patch a clover down at the vr end. Deer comes and sure loves that clover. Maybe thats where my Paw been dug and hes makin the clover real tasty to make up for all his killin.

Im bloated up like nobodies business. Fek I think Im goin have quads or somethin but the Doc says I jes normal like. She tells me its a girl. Im happy about that cause Im goin to call her Ruthie after my vr good friend. Sometimes when theres stars and that slivery moon I goes and sits on Ruthies rock. Its her rock now not Bobs. I gone put some babys breath in that rat hole. Rats hav run far probably sniffin out Bobs crumbly bones in the earth by the butterbeans. I talk to Ruthie on that rock and I tells her everthin. I tells her maybe Im a bloated up so big cause my baby got plenty to say jes like Ruthie said I did once. Still do I guess. Cody went got the typin machine when I told him I missed it. He wanted a buy me one them fancy computer boxes. I dont trust them. I like this old Smith and Jones contraption mighty fine. Cody says I should be a secretary one day ha ha. He even got me a book. Im no Mavis Beakon but Im learnin one finger at a time. Them numbers are hard fellas and that z and x and stuff.

I was tellin Ruthie about my talky little one thats goin to pop out sooner than later. I sure hopes so cause its like carrin a fekkin 3 quarter ton truck. I tell my vr good dead friend I figger my little Ruthie girl goin to have some good stories to tell for a change. Yes sir.

oh p.s.

I got me an other cow. She a beauty. I aint figgered a name yet but maybe shes jes called Petal too.

The Burning

- Mischa Hiller -

Helen's concentration was broken by the sound of Jack's key in the front door. She was standing at the kitchen table still in her work suit, reading a newspaper spread out flat before her. She tried to find her place in the article but it was too late; she was distracted by the noises Jack was making and her whole body clenched. The sound of the door closing, the thud of his case on the hall floor, the short scrape of the metal studs as he pushed it behind the door with his foot; there were marks on the wooden floor from eleven years of him doing that. Then came the rustle of his raincoat as he took it off. A grubby, stained raincoat he refused to replace, even though they could easily afford it. She heard his laboured breath as he bent to pick up his post where she had left it on the floor coming in. Worst of all though, was that inevitable sigh at some presumption, possibly the fact that his surname had been misspelt again or that he had received some harmless junk mail.

She tried to focus on the newspaper and read the last sentence again as he scuffed his heels into the kitchen. Even though her back was to him she could sense him standing at the door. She heard the rip of paper. It was an effort to raise her head and look round at him. Jack stood in the kitchen doorway in a grey suit that was shiny at the elbows. There was a new stain on the lapel. He was holding his post, reading one of the letters.

He raised his eyes to her and their gaze coincided briefly, too briefly for anything beyond acknowledgement to pass between them. He made a grunting noise and went back to his letter. Helen's eyes moved to his stomach, wider than his chest. As a cardiologist she knew it was a good predictor of heart attacks in men, having a waist bigger than the chest; it was the first thing she visually checked when male patients came into her clinic. She did not know when she had stopped caring about what had happened to Jack's stomach, or to his suit, or his filled-out face. She had loved his body once; she could still remember running her fingers over his taut stomach. But she had not done it for so long that it was a distant memory that might well relate to someone else she had once known. Helen turned back to her newspaper; the daylight was fading and soon one of them would have to put the light on.

She heard him replacing the letter in the envelope and he appeared in her peripheral vision and set his post on her open newspaper. Annoyed, she pushed the envelopes out of the way, even though they weren't covering what she was reading, and tried to find her place in the article, but he took the kettle and started filling it noisily at the sink.

'What are we eating?' he said, raising his voice above the sound of the water. Hearing another question in his tone she raised her eyes to the ceiling but it was lost on him as he wasn't looking.

'I've just got back myself, so whatever you can find,' she said. The strain leaked out through her voice, constrained by the tightness in her throat. The water stopped and she watched him put the kettle on the clear and shiny granite worktop and push the plug into its base. It clicked several times as he tried to turn it on and she stopped herself from correcting him about the switch: you had to press it gently, otherwise it just clicked back to the off position. It was one of those kettles that was supposedly designer, but without the functional robustness Jack expected from appliances. It was something she had bought when refurbishing the kitchen while on forced sick leave. Getting the kitchen upgraded had given her something to do, and reassured others that she could function. Jack, although happy to complain about the things she bought for the house, had never, in all the years they'd been together, bought an appliance himself.

She found her place in the newspaper and started to read from the start of the paragraph again, but now Jack was rummaging noisily in the fridge, clattering jars and examining foil containers of unidentifiable leftovers. She did not know why they kept the leftovers of their takeaway food, they never ate them, and were never at home during the day. She ate with colleagues in the hospital canteen, or popped onto the Fulham Road for a freshly filled baguette at that French sandwich place with them. She always ate in front of people, so they didn't wonder. She did not know what Jack did for lunch.

'Why do we keep these things?' She turned round and saw him tossing the containers onto the worktop next to the sink. He held one near her face. 'This has gone mouldy.' She ignored his attempt to get a rise out of her—his rough handling of the contents of the fridge, the unthinking assumption that she should be the one that dealt with its contents. Sticking the container in her face like that. She felt the anger rising within her and cut it off with a question.

'Where do you have lunch?' she asked.

'What?' Giving her a look suggesting she was stupid or was speaking a foreign language he hadn't quite got to grips with. It was a familiar look she had come to hate. There had been a time when it was funny but she could not pinpoint the moment when it had no longer become so. Probably when she had stopped caring that he was overweight or when he had told her that he didn't want children. She perched against the edge of the kitchen table and pulled at a hangnail. All her nails were bitten short and there were shreds of raw flesh at the roots where she had pulled strips of skin off. Her thin fingers were covered in sagging translucent skin, like poorly filled chipolatas.

'I'm just asking what you do for lunch every day?'

'I eat a sandwich at my desk usually, from the university canteen. I don't know, does it matter?' Helen tugged at a bit of nail with her teeth. His dopey, fat assistant probably bought his lunch for him, he being too busy with his stupid research to even think of eating. He expected all practical things to be done for him; it was a marvel that he was able to make tea. The kettle started to heat up the water inside it and although she was a science graduate Helen did not know why it should make more noise as it got hotter. Was it the steam building up inside the kettle, the expansion of water molecules? He would know of course, but to ask him would mean deferring to his knowledge, and she was determined never to do that. Jack closed the fridge and with its small light extinguished Helen became aware of how dark it was getting. She didn't want to switch the main light on because it would mean squeezing past Jack. He went to the cupboard and looked inside, as if a ready-made meal might jump out at him. She wasn't sure why he was bothering with this charade; all he had to do was choose one of the many menus they had pinned on the cork board. It was what they did when they were here, unless he was at some function, in which case she didn't have to eat, and could relish that gnawing feeling in her hungry gut. Helen saw that his trousers were worn thin at the seat, and that folds of cloth hung over the top of his scuffed shoes. He may be a brilliant man, but he was no dresser. She smiled at this observation, made herself chuckle out loud, but he didn't ask what was funny.

The kettle, reaching a crescendo of boiling and spluttering, clicked loudly and settled down. Pulling out a chair Helen sat at the table and looked at the newspaper but could no longer make out the words.

'Put the light on, will you?' she asked. He said nothing but closed the cupboard and went to the teapot and put a teabag in it, then switched the kettle on again to reboil the water. She watched his back as he stood there, his hand on the kettle, waiting for it to reboil; he refused to pour non-boiling water onto his teabag, a quirk he had when they'd met fourteen years ago. The anger expanded within her, and she counted her breath, four seconds in, four seconds out, breathing from the diaphragm, as the therapist had suggested. 'People forget to breathe when they are angry. By counting as you inhale and exhale, you will remember to breathe and this will automatically slow your heart rate.'

But her breathing exercise was no match for the knowledge that Jack had deliberately ignored her request to put the light on. How childish he was, how arrogant. The emotion welled up again, threatening to escape. She tried another trick taught by the therapist: concentrating on the detail of something outside what was going on in her head. She looked at the letters he had put on the table; the only one he had opened had a Swedish postmark. She hoped it was another conference; a few days with the flat to herself would be a relief. The kettle clicked and she watched him pour spluttering, boiling water into the teapot, and had a fleeting, pleasing vision of him scalding himself and her having to take him to hospital. She looked down at her shredded fingertips. She wanted a cup of tea but could not ask for one; the request was lodged in her chest and would not come out. Instead, she would wait and see if he would pour her one, as a test, a measure of his contempt for her. Part of her wanted him not to pour one, so that she would be right about his feelings for her. She turned to look out of the window, but it was getting dark, and what she saw was the ghostly reflection of a narrow face and wrinkled forehead; a rigid face, rigid with...with what? She looked away, hating the features enlarged by her sunken cheeks. Jack turned to face her, waiting for the tea to brew, leaning against the counter, crossing his arms. She looked at him and his gaze dropped to the table.

'What's with Sweden?' she asked, tapping the envelope, hoping again for some days alone at home. He shifted on his feet and then moved to the light switch by the door, catching his heels on the tiles. It would leave marks that she would scrub out when he had gone to bed.

'It's a prize, for the research.' He switched the lights on and she looked at the envelope with new interest as it was highlighted by a spot in the ceiling.

'You've won a prize?'

'For the stem cell research,' he said, coming back to the counter. He had mentioned it before, and she recalled that it had some bearing on her own work as a cardiologist, but she didn't understand it, hadn't even tried to understand it. It was a world he could not share with her, a world with no place for children.

'What does it mean?' she asked. He went back to the counter and stirred the tea. He half-turned his head but kept his eyes on the teapot.

'What, the research?' She picked up the envelope—was he deliberately trying to provoke her by being obtuse? The emotion rose again and this time she could not contain it.

'You know what I bloody mean. I mean is there a presentation, some funding attached, a fucking medal?' Something on a shelf resonated to her shrill sarcasm, one of the matching but empty containers that should hold rice and sugar and flour, but had never been filled.

'Yes, yes, of course. It will attract funding to the university,' he quickly said. His hand moved to the rack and, ignoring the set of expensive mugs she had bought to match the rest of the crockery, took down a chipped and tea-stained mug. She believed he kept it just to annoy her. On it was written: 'Boffins do it in white coats'. She'd bought it for him five years ago from a joke shop on the King's Road, when she'd still thought being a research scientist was cool, a hidden world where unsung heroes did unacknowledged work.

While he was pouring his tea she prised apart the envelope opening so she could see inside. An embossed, gilt-edged invitation card was sitting on top of a letter and by angling the envelope, she could read the cursive script. It invited Jack and a guest to a black-tie dinner and presentation at the Stockholm Sheraton on 23rd October. The gurgle of pouring tea stopped and she quickly put the envelope back. Her heart was thudding as he turned round, although it was unlikely he would notice that the envelope had moved; such mundane things fell outside the scope of his attention.

He moved to the table, steaming mug in hand, and picked up his letters. She could smell his tea but no longer cared about getting any, about being right. The invitation crowded all that out. She started to count her breath but then he was moving to the door and she was forced to speak before he left the room.

'When's the ceremony?' she asked. He stopped and looked at her and for some reason he was staring at her mouth.

'You're biting your nails again,' he said. Helen yanked her fingers from her teeth and buried them in her armpit. She could feel the sweat through the material of her jacket. He let out a sigh and she saw a triumphant, condescending smile on his fat lips and in one movement rose from her seat, swinging a clenched hand at his face. His eyes flared and he stepped back, and her fist knocked his mug, sloshing hot tea onto her hand. She shrieked with the unexpected pain, then let out an angry scream into his shocked face.

'Oh God I'm sorry,' he was saying. 'I didn't mean...' She held her hand up and could see reddening and puckering skin. She wanted to cry with the pain but anger was still the greater emotion. He put the envelopes and mug down on the counter, took her by the wrist and led her to the sink. 'You should run it under cold water,' he said. He turned the tap on, let it run for a few seconds, then plunged her hand under the whooshing torrent. The icy water against the burning made her gasp, but the shock of it overcame the scald and swamped her rage like the anti-depressants never did; they only seemed to obscure it in a numbing fog, which is why she had stopped taking them. There was a suffusion of warmth in her brain, a massive release of endorphins, and the clinician in her understood that it was caused by the burn and the cold water.

Breathing in quick puffs she looked up at the window over the sink. It was now completely dark outside and all she could see was Jack and her at the sink. Jack was looking back at her in the reflection. They held each other's gaze and somehow it was easier to do so in the glass than face to face. The water got colder and her hand grew numb but he held her wrist in a firm grip in case she might snatch it from the flow. The only sound was of the water splashing onto the stainless steel. He looked down at her hand and so did she. They hadn't been this physically close for several months, not even in bed. She felt serene, almost content. Quietly, she said, 'You're not taking me to Stockholm with you, are you?' He turned off the tap and examined her hand tenderly, as if it were a wounded bird.

'You'll live,' he said, letting go of it.

'Just tell me,' she said. It was no effort to keep her voice soft, no effort at all. He looked at her as if to read her face and she understood that he was afraid. Afraid of her. 'It's OK,' she said. He turned his hands to show her his palms, as if to convince her he had nothing to hide.

'I'm sorry, Helen.' His face dropped in resignation and weariness and her eyes stung with tears.

'No,' she said. 'I'm the one who should be sorry.' Her hand started to burn again but it was a good feeling, a real feeling, one to savour and keep.

The Latvian Motorcycle Princess

- C. D. Rose -

The Latvian Motorcycle Princess rides her dreams across vast empty spaces, no destination other than the limitless horizons of her imagination. Every day she cruises through wide flat fields, riding the light from dawn to dusk, watching for the moment when the huge skies briefly turn the colour of tail-lights. The Latvian Motorcycle Princess leans back, feels the roar of her engine, the gentle burn of exhaust and breathes in the motorcycle emptiness of the open roads, dreaming racetracks and laurel wreaths, spuming magnums of champagne, flame-retardant Belstaff leathers and extensive sponsorship deals. The Latvian Motorcycle Princess ignores roadsigns, closes her eyes and dreams of walls of death, leaping canyons and endless wheelies. Such dreams help the Latvian Motorcycle Princess to ignore the fact she no longer lives in Latvia and does not yet live in Los Angeles. At this current moment, the Latvian Motorcycle Princess lives in Thetford.

The Latvian Motorcycle Princess was Riga and District under 16 BMX champion five years running, up until the point she was no longer under 16 and there were no more championships for her to enter. It was then, perhaps, that she first thought of heading west. The Latvian Motorcycle Princess had always dreamed of leaving, even in the times when it was so much more difficult than today. But it wasn't the grubby reveries of easy riches or high ideals of personal freedom that made her dream, she had no desire to shop Manhattan dry, dine on *foie gras* on the Champs Elysee or broker marriage with minor titles in Belgravia. The Latvian Motorcycle Princess wanted nothing but horsepower, torsion, throttle, endless front forks and a low centre of gravity. The Latvian Motorcycle Princess wanted two wheels, speed, the wind in her hair and the purr of one twentyfive, two fifty, threefifty, five hundred cubic centilitres of engine.

The Latvian Motorcycle Princess dreams the world in terms motorcyclical and in her dreams she crosses the Gulf of Bothnia and heads for the midnight sun on a Husqvarna, cruises around old Prague and Cesky Budowice on a vintage CSA. In her head the Latvian Motorcycle Princess rolls a Ducati through rolling Tuscan hills, takes the hairpins of the Amalfi coast road on a Moto Guzzi, her hair unpinned, charms boys, girls and traffic police while endlessly looping the Colosseum on a Gilera. She circles snowtopped Fuji on a Kawasaki, darts through the Roppongi rush hour on a Suzuki, visits geishas and geysers on a Yamaha, rides out Hokusai waves on a Honda. The Latvian Motorcycle Princess takes the autobahn trans-Europe on a smoothly-sprung BMW, but most of all she glides through the heat haze of an endless Arizona desert highway on a Harley, Harley, Harley Davidson.

When The Latvian Motorcycle Princess had an opportunity to go to Britain, her comrades talked of bowler-hatted gentlemen and tattooed football hooligans, of tea and rain, of Di and Camilla. But the Latvian Motorcycle Princess thought of nothing other than racing green Triumphs through green hills, taking Silverstone's chicanes or Donington's podium on a Norton, winding round country houses and crumbling castles on a BSA. But the Latvian Motorcycle Princess has found Britain disappointing; as she idles along the A11 from Attleborough to Snetterton at a modest thirty, the Latvian Motorcycle Princess rides a moped.

I didn't see her until it was too late. I never bother looking both ways, least of all in Thetford. I just stepped right out and there she was, only just chugging twenty, but still enough to hit me. I'd like to think her lithe, quicksilver speed sliced through my peripheral vision, but given the state of the thing she was riding, it seems improbable. Soldered together from hooky parts that had been seeking asylum in a friendly junkyard or escaping from a detention centre for knock-off rustbuckets, with license plates assembled from a B&Q Letraset and an engine better suited to a hair-dryer, her ride had been reanimated by a Polish guy smelling of pickles and homebrew vodka who everyone called Jan. (Not his real name, but as his real name was even more difficult to pronounce than it was to spell, 'Jan' stuck). She'd bought the moped for the price of a shag, but had at least managed to get it on credit, gambling on Jan not being round for long enough to call in his debts.

'Understeer,' she said, and I thought it was some kind of insult aimed at me, only later realising that it was her way of apologising. Her vocabulary rarely stretched to more than the purely technical: she'd learned all the English she knew from Haynes manuals and *The Observer's Guide to Classic Motorcycles*. The only thing I ever heard her say, in fact, that had nothing to do with two-stroke torsion were the words: 'What is your name?', and even those, of course, though she was not yet to know it, were also motorcyclical.

I didn't know then the one thing that could make her stop more quickly than well-oiled ABS disc brakes. If I had known I may have been a little more circumspect about revealing my name. I could have just told her I was Mr. Davidson, a surname as bland as white-sliced, and about as unusual. Where my first name came from is still a mystery to me: the closest my dad ever got to a motorbike was buying some Brut 33 because Barry Sheene advertised it on telly, though I could never be quite so sure about my mum, who often made hints about a misspent quarter of an hour with the kind of boys who knew just a bit too much about Brylcreem. Whatever, I believe it was my parents' misplaced attempts to give me some personality that had led them to christen me *Harvey*. I've never known if that one wrong letter was my parents' attempts to lend a little individuality to my name or, more likely, a mistake on the part of my half-cut father at the maternity ward.

For the Princess, however, my name worked like the keys to the ignition: once given, she told me of her days—her hands up chickens' bottoms while dreaming of the wind in her hair, grit in her face, the smell of brake fluid and the squeal of burning rubber, sump oil and two-stroke in the pores of her skin. Most of the Poles, Portuguese, Lithuanians, Moldavians and Ukrainians with whom she worked were proud of what they did, counted the number of chickens plucked, gutted and stuffed everyday as a symbol of their fortitude, but not her. All she wanted to do was rev up, and roll away.

In the East Anglian summer the days seem like they may go on forever and the sky is so far away that she can easily think she is back in Latvia with her grandfather in their dacha by the sea. As a child she passed mosquito-filled summers in high damp grass near Ventspils, close enough to the water to get a drift of the corrosive salt wind that blew a layer of damp under all the mattresses, though not quite close enough to see the cold Baltic. There was always the smell of rotting apples, pears or plums which her aunt attempted to turn into improbably strong liqueurs or, failing that, jam, though in the end the two were often indistinguishable.

Her Grandfather Aleksander still privately insisted they weren't Latvian but *echt Deutsch*, though he never said this publicly. After the war, it was far safer to be Russian than German. He never spoke Latvian, only Russian to her when she went to see what he was doing in his shed at the bottom of the dacha's endless garden (though 'shed' was hardly the right word, the dacha itself being little other than a shed with a privy).

'*Putnins,*' he said to her. 'The greatest Latvian motorcycle.' Grandfather Aleksander claimed to have one of the few models left in working order. 'They had a factory in Riga,' he told her. 'A palace of engineering marvels.' She imagined the Putnins factory, dreamed it anew where it had once been, near the tower block where she now lived, a place of Wonka-ish wonder. She loved the piece of iron and rubber that was the old motorcycle as much as Grandfather Aleksander did, its smell of paint and rust and oil and petrol.

Her Grandfather had once owned a bicycle shop, or at least that's what he'd told her, and then, usually after two or three drops of Grandma's liqueur, claimed that he had taken the step of adding a lawnmower engine to one of his pushbikes, thus himself having been responsible for the invention of the motorcycle. She knew he was lying, but it didn't matter. He was even proud that Putnins had then stolen the idea from him. Even though she knew he was lying, the idea that the motorcycle was an essentially Latvian invention had lodged itself firmly in her brain.

Grandfather Aleksander leant over and called her *принцесса*, telling her to lean at the precise moment they turned corners tight or wide as she clung on to the metal edges of the home-made canvas sidecar he bolted on to the 1938 Putnins every summer, just for her. They chugged and spluttered and rattled around the sea roads as far as the little towns that littered the coasts where they had to be quiet and not speak to each other other than through glances and signs and whispers. Now, it was dangerous to speak Russian: the time a fizzy splot of sputum had landed on grandfather's jacket after someone had overheard them stuck with her.

She would spend hours on the cold beaches with her grandfather, rooting through the debris among the rocks, picking up any kind of murky yet promising-looking stone, fishing for amber. They greeted the occasional German tourists warmly, though she remembers that her Grandfather was not able to speak to them, either.

Every year there was a rally in Kurland, a procession of vintage motorcycles from all over Europe and beyond. Grandfather Aleksander talked of it incessantly and she would always listen until the year eventually arrived in which she was old enough to persuade him to take her. They greased and oiled the Putnins, bolted the sidecar on, and set slowly out on their way. An eighty year-old man riding a seventy year-old motorbike travel slowly, especially when accompanied by a homemade sidecar carrying a now twenty-five year-old granddaughter. It took them a day to get to Slokenbeck, and by the time they arrived there, everyone else had left.

'No matter,' insisted Grandfather Aleksander. 'We will continue to the next stop and catch up with everyone there.' A day later, they found everyone had already left again, and they were a day late for the next three days, travelling only to find the occasional discarded tyre, faulty sparkplug or shard of broken wing mirror.

It was after that that she had decided to go to Thetford.

I didn't see her until it was too late: a week after I'd met her she was gone, and I'll never know where. She told me her tales and left. Maybe her visa ran out, maybe she never had one, maybe she's back in Riga now, or on her way there, crossing the sea or stuck on an overcrowded bus in the north of Poland. Maybe she was gangmastered to harvest organic purple endive in a vast polythene greenhouse, or subcontracted to a subcontractor who has her plucking even more disease-ridden chickens for a major supermarket chain near a town even sadder than Thetford. Or maybe she finally got to ride that Harley.

Turtle

- Melinda Moore -

Kitty had never really considered how often people died. There seemed to be no end to the stream of covered bags being wheeled into the Funeral Parlour. She craned forward out of the window, her chest pressed uncomfortably hard against the thin metal frame, and peered into the narrow street below. The sun beat down on her nose and forehead, adding to her despised freckle collection—little flecks of melanin, like the floaters in her eye: a constant irritant since she had ignored Dad's instruction not to stare up at the sun. Even the roar of traffic seemed muted, as wheels thrummed on melting tarmac, its pungent smell masking the usual sulphurous tang of seaweed. The seagulls' frantic cawing seemed to have calmed to a lazy, sporadic squawk and, over the screams of other children in the park nearby, Kitty could hear, as always, the sound of sawing. Shading her eyes with her hand, she watched as faint clouds of sawdust rose from the workshop below, floating rapidly upwards and then slowing and circling in the currents of hot air that lay low over the streets and the town. There was no discernible breeze.

There wasn't even a breeze at sea, Kitty's father had said. He was back on land after three weeks spent diving in the murk of Blackpool Bay, retrieving lead from a ship downed by its crew's inattention. A giant turtle had been seen floating, unconcerned, far from its normal hunting grounds, lured into the bay by unusually warm weather and a shifting Gulf Stream. Whilst the ship's crew scrambled for a sight of the mammoth shell with its strange head, wrinkled like a cancer patient or premature baby, no-one remembered to take depth soundings, nor did they watch for the spines of the rocks. Later, when all bar the captain were safe on land, foil-wrapped and with paramedics all around, they were still full of what they had seen.

The captain's body was discovered two days later—a swollen carapace out in open water, rising and falling with the swell. He was drifting face down, eye sockets turned towards the depths. He would not be much missed: Dad said he had never been popular, driving his crew too hard and often allowing greed to put their lives at risk. The turtle had disappeared by then.

Of course, the captain had died in Blackpool and so wouldn't be lying downstairs being measured for his coffin: oak for display, pine for economy. Nevertheless, he could be said, Kitty supposed, to be as much a victim of the heat as all the bag-wrapped bodies lying some ten feet below where she was standing. His loss proved her father's gain. First to lay claim to the ship, Dad had been away even longer than usual, stripping the boat of everything that could be sold on, working in dangerous cross-currents, and posting one of his crew on deck day and night, both to guard the divers working on the ocean floor, and to protect his salvage rights against what he called 'bloody buccaneers'.

For three weeks, the people of Milford Haven had been dying like flies. In fact, Kitty thought, they had been dying *instead* of the flies, which flew repeatedly around her face in what she considered deliberate attempts to annoy her. Kitty wondered where the dead people slept downstairs until their boxes were made. Were there rows of beds on the floor below where she stood now, or did the undertaker prop the bodies up somehow against the walls? Was it boring being dead? Her stepmother, Babs, refused to answer such questions, refused to even think about what went on beneath their flat—though Kitty noticed that she always crossed herself whenever she heard the workshop door slide back or the purr of one of the big sleek black cars that came to collect the coffins.

Kitty loved to watch the cars drive off from the Chapel of Rest, though she couldn't quite see the point of having such expensive ones, when they only ever went at about ten miles an hour. She knew her father thought it a waste, too. He was always muttering, 'Rolls Royce engine at *that* speed' before he got into his own Morris Traveller. Kitty thought she would like a big beautiful car to take her on her last journey, but she intended to leave strict instructions that it was to be driven at one hundred miles an hour. The time saved would be used to drive her up and down the seafront a few times before going on to the church. That way she could say goodbye to the sea.

Kitty had it all planned: the hymns; the poems; who would speak about how wonderful she, Kitty, had been, and who was required to cry loudly and publicly. Morbid, her stepmother called it. Prescient, said Kitty, who had been given a copy of the *Oxford English Dictionary* for her birthday. She loved to learn new words and studying the dictionary late at night gave her an advantage over her father during the impromptu spelling tests he would give her whenever he took her down to the docks with him to help on the boat.

'I can do harder ones than that, Dad,' she would say, and he would rack his brains to try to beat her.

So far, Kitty had only been beaten once—and that was when Dad had cheated by looking up scientific words and telling her to spell deoxyribonucleic acid. She did need to be a bit more careful with the dictionary study, though. Pronunciation was such a problem if you had only read the word and had never heard it said.

Mrs Johnson at school had laughed, quite cruelly Kitty thought, when Kitty had pronounced 'moccasin' as 'mow-*cass*-in' when the class were talking about Red Indians last term. Kitty's face had gone as red as her hair, even through the horrible freckles. That night, she had got her father to explain the little clues in brackets that showed you how to pronounce words, and now she practised her new ones in private, until she was sure they would not let her down.

There were lots of words that applied to dead people in the dictionary. Morbidity; rigor mortis; departed, late—Kitty thought that one ridiculous, as surely never ever turning up again was slightly more than just *late*. Necrophilia sounded repulsive and she was sure that the dictionary meaning must be wrong, but she hadn't managed to ask Dad yet as she hadn't been able to get him on his own since he got back last night. He'd just gobbled his tea, ruffled her on the head and kissed her stepmother—and then gone out 'to see a man about a dog'.

Kitty had gone to bed as usual, only to be woken by Babs much later and told to get up and put on her dressing gown and slippers. All Kitty's questions were ignored, and Babs had said, in a chokey sort of voice, 'you're too young to be left here by yourself. Just do as I tell you.'

They went out into the car park at the rear of the flats and got into the car. Babs drove out past the funeral parlour, but so fast that Kitty only caught a glimpse of the big wooden door to the workshop, almost as tall as the whole of the ground floor. She thought she saw a glimmer of light around the edge, so maybe they left a light on in case any of the dead people were scared of the dark.

The wide streets of Milford Haven were deserted as Babs drove on, first down the hill that bisected Charles Greville Hamilton's perfect gridiron design, and then turning right onto Hamilton Terrace, named by the architect for his cuckolded uncle's wife Emma, Nelson's great love. The town hall clock showed a quarter past four, and the streets of white houses were in darkness but, as ever, a myriad of small lights twinkled on the pulsing obsidian of the water. The sweep of the beam from the St Anne's Head lighthouse lit the entrance to the harbour, before turning its eye back out to sea, repeatedly tracing the curve of the bay.

Babs drove past the Nelson Hotel and, almost skidding on the bend, took a sharp left into the docks. The car's headlights briefly illuminated the sign: *Milford Haven Port Authority Welcomes Careful Drivers.* As they passed the dry dock, the huge dark stern of a ship reared up skywards from its deep concrete bathtub, casting its vast shadow over the car and momentarily obscuring the moonlit silhouette of Babs's set face. Kitty sat tight in the passenger seat as Babs drove too fast towards the unlit edge of the harbour, a scream welling up in her chest as she anticipated the plunge from solid ground to oil-black water; but then the car stopped, inches from the perimeter, and Kitty opened the door and staggered out, legs much shakier than after days at sea.

She looked up at the Port Authority office, expecting to see light through the skewed slats of the drooping venetian blinds. It was in darkness. Kitty had known that a night like tonight would happen eventually: she had rehearsed it so many times when lying in bed listening to the Shipping Forecast. Whenever the sonorous voice intoned 'Lundy, Fastnet, Irish Sea', and 'gale force winds', Kitty would lie awake for the rest of the night, waiting for the telephone to ring, or for a knock at the door. But, now that disaster had occurred, where were the officials? The harbourmaster? Had the lifeboat already been sent out? Seeking an explanation, Kitty turned to look for Babs, but she was already almost out of sight. Kitty could just see her nearing the bottom of the ladder fixed into the harbour wall, about to step onto the boat moored closest to it.

'Wait for me, Babs!' Kitty shouted, but her stepmother didn't answer, just gestured at Kitty to stay put—but this was Kitty's father who was missing at sea, feared drowned—so there seemed nothing for it but to start climbing down the slippery, algae-clad ladder herself.

Clambering over the moored boats in Babs's wake, dressing gown a fluffy pink hazard, Kitty tried to focus on her feet—chanting Dad's strict instruction to 'watch the ropes' under her breath. The rubber soles on her slippers had a reasonable grip, but the early dew was making the decks slippery, and the ebb and flow of the water caused the boats to shift constantly. Only those moored outside the harbour wall carried riding lights, and Kitty could barely see where to tread in the insipid light of the moon. She couldn't understand why Babs was wasting time with fishing boats when what was needed was a lifeboat, or a helicopter. Didn't she realise that if anything happened to Dad, Kitty would have to go back to live with Mum? No, she wouldn't think about that. If you thought about things, you might make them happen. Dad was a fighter—look at how he'd fought for custody—and luckily it was still warm, so maybe he could survive in the water for as long as it took for him to be rescued. Wasn't it warm water that had lured the turtle from its normal hunting grounds? Dad would be treading water like a turtle, waiting for help. He'd probably be spelling out words to pass the time.

Distracted, Kitty tripped, encumbered by her loose pyjama bottoms. Disentangling her feet, she glanced up just in time to see Babs opening the cabin door of the boat moored furthest out in the dock, a French trawler bearing the name, *Le Loup* and registered to Brest. As Kitty watched, a shaft of bright light shone out, seemingly carried on the wave of raucous laughter that rose from the cabin below and bounced over the dark water beyond. Babs disappeared from view and Kitty began to hurry after her, shivering, despite the still-warm air.

Today, Kitty was tired. It had been daylight when she went to bed. She yawned, slow and wide, before resting her forehead back against the window, her eyes watering. There was a sudden noise of something heavy being dragged, and the floor vibrated slightly. Surprised, Kitty jerked her head, banging it on the edge of the window frame. Her temple hurt and she rubbed the spot, a trace of blood showing on her fingers when she removed her hand. There was no longer anyone to ask for a plaster, so Kitty just rubbed again, and opened the window further, cautiously putting her head out through the gap. Then came the noise of an engine and one of the long black shiny cars turned into the street below. Pressing her hand to her head, she watched as a stretcher was wheeled out into the street, and up to the rear of the car. It bore a coffin, oak or even mahogany, although the sunlight reflecting off its highly-polished surface and ornate brass handles made it hard to tell. The black-coated men lifted the coffin and slid it, quite effortlessly, into the back of the car, then turned and went back inside. Kitty tried to imagine what it would be like inside that box in this heat. She hoped the lining would be cool. And soft.

And then the men were back, carrying armfuls of flowers, a garish carnival of colour—deep pinks, yellows that screamed in the sun, oscillating blues of every shade from cornflower to violet; most with small white envelopes poking out of their packaging on plastic sticks. Kitty chewed a strand of her hair and wondered whether the people who wrote those messages thought that the dead people would be able to read them. Did they think that the corpses would crawl out of their coffins at night and open all the envelopes and note down the names of the senders, like Babs did with the Christmas cards they received each year?

She remembered last night—the sound of women laughing; her father's voice, drunk and pleading, and then Babs's voice, screaming over and over again: 'I wish you were dead.' Then Babs's face, a wreck beyond salvage, as she had sat sobbing in the car after finally being brought back to shore.

Kitty slapped away the small black flies clustering around the cut on her head; heard footsteps turning the corner into the street and glanced to her left. An old man, so thin that his dark suit hung in loose folds from his shoulders like the pipes on the organ at church, walked slowly up to the black car. He carried a bunch of flowers, the like of which Kitty had never seen before. Long, long, pale green stems—spring green like fresh celery—gave way to slender, creamy-white trumpets, bowed down like the man's head—its pale pink, shiny skin with mottled brown patches showing through his sparse white hair. The man reached into the car and placed the flowers on top of the coffin: a pale, still centrepiece amidst the hectic turbulence of the cellophane-wrapped blooms that surrounded it. Then he closed the rear door and briefly rested his forehead against it. Kitty blinked as the man's shoulders shook under the too-big jacket. The engine started and he stood back to let the car pass, turning to follow it as it moved at a snail's pace towards the junction with the main road. Kitty watched as the man passed her window, pacing alone behind the hearse. A glint of sunlight on metal flashed in her eye as the man turned his wedding ring around on his finger, around and around, as he walked in his baggy suit on the hottest day of the year. Another fly dived at Kitty's face and—*slap!*—there it was, a thin, grey smear, just a trace on her palm.

Herringbone

- James Carter -

Where they have crouched and crawled and prayed
I stand, the self-doomed, unafraid,
Unfellowed, friendless and alone,
Indifferent as the herring-bone
(James Joyce, *The Holy Office*)

There comes a time for everyone when they must de-bone a herring.
(Delia Smith)

He remembered hearing once on a cookery programme a television chef
saying there is no such thing as a sardine, that what we buy as sardines are
just different types of herring. He had this in mind when he went to the
supermarket on the way home from work and brought some fresh
sardines. After the week he had just had he was looking for a way of
calling the bluff of whatever had been governing his experience for the
past seven days. Later when he opened the bag and looked at the fish for
the first time he regretted that a tin of pilchards would have done just as
well.

Using a sharp knife cut all along the bellies of the fish and remove the guts. Then chop off the heads and tails. Next, place the fish skin side up on a flat surface and press down firmly along the backbone with your thumb. Now turn over the fish and from the head end slowly peel the backbone away from the flesh.

He moved what was left of the fish to one side and brought up the corners of the sandwich bag which he had placed on top of his chopping board. He lifted the guts and put them into a second bag followed by the heads, tails and bones. Holding the bones for a moment it occurred to him just how featherlike they are. He tied up the bag and dropped it in the bin, and as he did this he considered some of the coincidences of the past week:

```
The T.V chef who said sardines are just different types of herring
Being awoken by herring gulls squawking loudly on the window ledge
In the underpass the fly posters advertising a Richard Herring gig
The herring Rolandsen plans to use in Knut Hamsun's novel Dreamers
The apologetic woman who sat opposite under a zigzag patterned hat
The odd telephone conversation considering the merits of roll mops
The herringbone trousers with braces Granddad wears during a visit
The story of the confused seal pup, scared of her plate of herring
Being given a 'herringbone' pot plant as a late house-warming gift
The soused herring outside co-op, being offered on cocktail sticks
The nature doc showing schools of herring in spectacular migration
The joke about Saint Aquino who opted for herring on his death bed
```

While some olive oil is heating in a frying pan, cover a plate with oatmeal. Now push the fillets onto the plate so they become well coated all over. Fry the fish on both sides for four minutes starting skin side down.

As he turned the fish over in the pan he tried to work out if there was a point where he had begun to look for what he was seeing and he cast his mind back a few days:

```
The complaint I misheard on the top deck: Her ring tone is rubbish
Cross-stitched coats, trousers, gloves, bags, skirts and cardigans
The brickwork I survey on my way along the high street twice a day
The woodblocks of various opulent floorings from galleries to pubs
The formation of cloud above like some variation on a mackerel sky
The hand-writing of the final letter of a long week in the archive
The oblique shape I see whilst looking afresh at my scarred finger
My eyes fix on a book stall display featuring an Op Art dust cover
Looking as the wind goes laconically by the leafless trees outside
```

Herringbone

```
Quizshow-snooker-food-talkinghead-lottery-ads-news-cartoonfishbone
Crouching to tie up my laces, I smile above the ubiquitous pattern
Abstracted by the linoleum floor, I lost my spot to a queue-jumper
```

'Fried Sardines in Oatmeal'. Season to taste and serve with wedges of lemon.

It didn't look much like the photo; he could see there were still a lot of fine bones in the flesh, but he was hungry now and the fish was tasty enough. If he hadn't seen them he would hardly have thought there was a bone left except for the few thicker ones which he separated with his teeth and placed around the edge of his plate. Looking at these more closely he laughed to himself when he saw he had arranged them in an awkward zigzag formation and he wondered if he was seeing things—the more ridiculous something becomes, the more remarkable it can be. Looking at the bones again, he thought over the past twenty-four hours where every surface had taken on the same pattern:

```
The dream I recorded in a note beside my bed stating herring gulls
The reflected pattern of my eyelashes as I put in my contact lens
The talk of DIY that reminded me of my childhood bedroom wallpaper
A feeling of déjà vu I experienced when mistook by a woman in a hat
The wrinkles down the face of an elderly woman as I travel to work
The herringbone I imagine, projected onto every surface and screen
The moon that lit up the sky with herringbone and covered the city
Choking on a stray bone in my sardine which I might've seen coming
```

Choking and collapsed, the plate smashed beside him; the last thing he felt was the herringbone at the back of his throat.

Post Day

- Lora Stimson -

I am sitting at the top of the apple tree, up higher than I usually go. So high that when the breeze shifts, I feel my stomach lurch. The leaves shimmy, their shadows dancing bruise-coloured across my skin. It's hot out on the lawn but up in the tree it's cool and damp as a fridge. I watch as my brother Max walks across the patio and out towards the greenhouse. I watch him take a joint from his shorts' pocket. When he reaches the greenhouse he lights it, leaning against the doorjamb. He thinks no one knows he smokes.

I'm bored. It's Friday, post day. All week Mum stacks the post on the kitchen table. She usually opens it on Friday afternoons. As I get home from school she'll be drinking a glass of wine, slitting the belly of each envelope with a kitchen knife. But she does things differently in the school holidays. Lets me eat dinner at four in the afternoon, or eleven at night.

The leaves suddenly shudder. Sunlight winks between them. Max squashes the butt of his joint underfoot; the last of the smoke rises and disappears above the greenhouse roof. He doesn't go back indoors but walks around the side of the house and out the front. There's nothing left to watch except the sun-scorched lawn. A little brown bird hops across it, cocking its head in quick, miniscule movements, listening at the ground. It plucks hopefully at a blade of grass and skips off. I climb down the tree. The dark end of the garden is full with green smells. I move out of the shade and cross the lawn. Everything is sizzling.

I'm not wearing shoes but wipe my feet on the doormat anyway. Mum isn't in the kitchen. I go along the hall. I don't shout in case Mum's sleeping. There's nothing she hates more than being woken. She sleeps with her wrists bent, her hands tucked in towards her. When she wakes, she unfurls like a flower. Reminds me of a bud opening, time-lapsed in a nature programme. I walk across the hallway's bare boards. Last September Mum took the carpet up. I remember this because it was my first day at Grovestone. When I came home the hallway furniture was on the front lawn and she was standing inside the front door with her hands on her hips, frowning. She said she would hire a sander and then varnish them. After a couple of days the bookshelf and standard lamp and shoe rack were moved back indoors. She never got around to sanding the floorboards. There's a sticky black margin round the edge of the hallway. A gummy no-go zone. The boards in the middle of the floor have big gaps between them. Mum says it's rustic. I just think it's embarrassing. Last week I found Max lying with his face against one of the cracks. He'd lost something between them but wouldn't tell me what. Later on, I took the torch from under the kitchen sink to investigate but all I saw was deposits of dust.

Pete's hallway carpet is thick and beige. His mum Hoovers it every day. Pete says it must be great having a spontaneous mother. He says it's no fun having dinner at the same time each day. He says his mum is too uptight. So uptight that she even irons the tea towels. He thinks it must be great to have a mum that never irons. On Pancake Day Pete's mum made drop scones. I sat at the kitchen table watching a globule of syrup roll slowly down the side of its glass bottle and just before it met the table, Pete's mum swept in with a wet cloth and wiped it away. I don't think my Mum would have even noticed. It would have sat in the middle of the table slowly hardening until it had become a part of the table top's terrain.

Mum isn't in the sitting room, or the study, which isn't a study at all but the place where she keeps things that don't belong anywhere else; boxes of floor tiles from when she thought about re-tiling the downstairs bathroom; a dressmakers mannequin; about a million of my old children's books that she refuses to throw out.

I move softly up the stairs, balancing on the balls of my feet. Sunlight rolls down the landing in a long orange stripe. Mum's bedroom door is open and I'm surprised to find her sitting at the end of her bed. I stand in the doorway and go to say something but pause. There is a strange feeling in the air, as if the room is holding its breath. Her hands are flat on her lap. It's not like Mum to be still. She's always moving, always occupied. I feel awkward. As if I've seen something I shouldn't have. Pete told me that he once walked in on his parents doing it.

Mum's crying. I can't actually see her crying but she exhales a small, shivery breath. She wipes her face and as she moves her head, notices me. I expect her to smile. To shake it off like she usually does. Especially on post day. Instead, she faces me, wearing an expression that I don't recognise, and turns back, not saying anything. I wonder if I should speak, or if I should just go to my bedroom. I twist my hands together.

'Are you OK, Mum?' I say it so suddenly that I surprise myself.

'Of course not,' she says. She releases a long breath.

'Do you need anything?'

'I need...' She rubs her palms up and down her lap. 'I need...' She stops and drops her head back. She's looking at the ceiling. The ceilings in our house have horrible swirling patterns scraped into them.

'No,' she says. 'I don't need anything, please just go away.'

It occurs to me that she might be ill. I stand for a moment lost in a horrifying daydream about Mum or Max dying, wondering what would happen to me. Whether I would have to go and live with Aunt Virginia, who isn't really my aunt at all but was married to someone who would have been my uncle, if he hadn't died before I was born. They'd never let me live with Grandpa, since he's an anarchist. Mum has friends I could go and stay with but I wouldn't actually like to live with any of them; they all smoke too much and hug too hard.

'Frances,' Mum snaps.

I twitch and go quickly to my room.

I scramble into bed and pull the covers over my head. My breath is amplified. I want to cry but instead concentrate on my breathing. It's small and close-up. After a while I sit up and wrap the duvet across my shoulders. I pick up the alarm clock by my bed and hurl it against my bedroom door. It makes a pathetic smash and pieces of it ping off across the room. Mum doesn't come to see what's happening. Not even to shout at me. I walk back downstairs, letting my feet thump against the steps and along the bare hallway boards. In the kitchen the post is still piled up unopened on the kitchen table. I get my bike from the shed and cycle to Pete's house.

I haven't seen Pete since the summer holiday's started. When we started Grovestone last year, Pete said that we'd probably stop being good friends. Because of the gender difference. He never referred to gender difference before. Pete has four brothers. I can't imagine living with that many boys. They live in a small pebbledash house. His younger brother Michael once squashed me against the outside wall and I had an imprint of those pebbles in my cheek all afternoon.

Pete isn't in. His dad has taken him fishing at the reservoir, his Mum tells me. We usually go fishing together.

'Isn't it illegal to fish at the reservoir?' I ask her.

She stands inside the front door bouncing baby Jason on her hip. She says she doesn't know. I don't say goodbye. I cycle home. I feel horrible inside, like I have an itch in my chest cavity. I sling my bike on the driveway. Mum hates this. Ever since she ran her Citroen over my old bike I have strict instructions to lean it up against a wall or put it away in the shed.

I don't want to go into the house. I think about Mum sitting on her bed and the itchy feeling inside my chest gets worse. I decide to go to the camp. We haven't been to the camp for a year. Not since Pete decided camps and bikes were childish. I don't see how wanting a place of your own is childish.

The camp is just a dip, a ditch between two fields out the back of my house. It's close enough to walk to but far away enough to feel like another country. There are small trees on either side, whose branches meet in the middle, creating a tunnel. There is a wooden bench and an old fruit crate to sit on. I can't remember what we did the last time we were there. It feels so long ago. Feels like it wasn't me but a different version of me, a twin I've since lost.

Approaching, I can hear voices. I wonder if Pete is not fishing at all but there with his new school friends. Now the itch is a violent tremble. I realise that the voices are adult and one is laughing, a fluttery female laugh. The other voice belongs to Max. I turn dark purple inside. Max is determined to invade every space. Ever since he came home from university last month he's been leaving trails of himself all through the house. Abandoned cereal bowls, wet towels on the bathroom floor. Bicycle parts sitting on the kitchen worktops like useless sculptures. He has re-tuned Mum's car stereo and in the evenings roots himself to the sofa. Our TV doesn't have a remote and he makes me get up to switch channels.

I can see him. He has his back to me. He's smoking a joint. He's always smoking a joint. He passes it to the girl next to him. More like a woman. She is older than Max, almost as old as Mum. Mum was only twenty when she had Max. The woman has taken her shoes and socks off and is wearing bracelets that jangle as she raises the joint to her mouth. She throws her head back and exhales a cloud. Max leans forward and kisses her. I take a step back. I am behind a spindly tree and at any moment they might see me. I shouldn't be watching them. I know this. I carry on watching. The woman drops the joint and clutches my brother's face. The joint produces a perfectly straight line of smoke. They kiss like they are in a film. Like they are eating ice-cream. They are making appreciative *mmmm* noises. They slip messily to the floor. The smoke is disturbed and sent into untidy coils. Max is putting his hand up her skirt. I feel like Pete when he found his parents doing it. My heart is hammering so loud that I'm worried they might hear it. My brother jerks against her and the woman takes a loud gulp of air.

I turn and run as fast as I can. My heart is a pulse, pulse, pulse in my ears. I race through the field snatching handfuls of the long meadow grass. In the middle of the field I stop. The blood in my ears slows to a thump. I pick the seeds from a stalk of grass and lay them on my flattened palm. A few are disturbed by the breeze and shudder as if they are alive. I blow across my palm and they spin off. Birds babble above me. Somewhere in the grass near me a cricket chirrups. Everything is fizzing.

At home Mum has closed her bedroom door. I imagine her sleeping, curled like a cat. Beyond my bedroom window the sun is beginning to dip behind the apple tree at the dark end of the garden. A huge blue shadow casts itself across the lawn. Hot orange light spills over my bedroom floor and makes something there glint. It's part of my alarm clock, a small metal ring. A sad, hollow feeling spreads across me. I collect the remains and lay them out like a museum display. I imagine the placard:

Alarm Clock—c.1993
Remains of an alarm clock destroyed by anger in the August Outburst of 1994. The batteries ran out two months before the clock was destroyed but it is thought they were never replaced.

I gather the small metal parts and pieces of shattered plastic and throw them into my desk drawer. I hear Mum's bedroom door open. She moves along the landing. I hold my breath. She pauses for a moment then descends the stairs. Her feet tap a hollow rhythm across the hallway floorboards.

When I go to the kitchen she's not there. I press my nose against the patio doors; I see her at the dark end of the garden, smoking a cigarette amongst the trees. She thinks I don't know that she sometimes smokes. She has her back to me, wearing a cardigan that is far too thick for the weather. When her cigarette is done she fishes a packet from her cardigan pocket and lights another. I want to be there with her, smoking and laughing at the bottom of the garden. I don't like smoking but I like the smell of it in the air. I wonder how long she'll stay down there. I wonder if Max will come home tonight, or if anyone will make dinner. I suddenly realise how hungry I am and find myself wishing that Mum had made Summer Bake, which is a mixture of pasta and anything leftover in the fridge and is always different and always the most delicious food I have ever tasted.

I take a knife from the draining board and sit at the kitchen table. I look at the pile of post. I imagine cutting each letter into tiny squares and posting each one between the gaps in the hallway floorboards. Imagine them fluttering like confetti into the dusty void between each board. Instead, I slice each envelope open and sort them into groups; Bill, Statement, Junk, Other. In the garden, Mum is now standing in the middle of the lawn with her head tipped back, letting the last of the sunshine warm her face.

Waiting Room

- Martin Pond -

I've never been anywhere that is so white.

The walls are white, the ceiling's white, the floor is all white tiles. The door in the far wall is white too. Even the magnetic lock thing that holds it shut is white.

In fact, the only thing that isn't white is the bench I'm sat on. That's stainless steel and it's not really a bench, it's just a long slab that sticks out of the wall. The edge is hurting the back of my legs.

I've been waiting about twenty minutes now. Well, I think so, they took my watch and phone off me when they signed me in, so I'm guessing but that's how long it feels like. I said to Mum that we shouldn't have got here so early but Dad got stroppy and said it was important and that every little thing could count towards the result. It didn't hurt to be early, he said, not when every little thing counts.

I wish I knew more about what was going to happen next. Danny Roberts, he's in my English class and he's two days older than me, so he took his Test on Tuesday. I blipped him that afternoon and he got it, I know cos I put a receipt on it and that came back straight away. But he didn't answer. I blipped him again yesterday, telling him not to be tight and to give me some clues about the Test, but I got a network error telling me the blip was undeliverable. Maybe he's changed his phone.

I've more or less given up asking Mum and Dad about it, and why it's so important. That's cos every time I asked one or other of them would get angry. It's alright when Dad shouts but when Mum does she goes red and shakes and I don't like that, so I don't ask any more. All Dad would say is that if they tell me about it the Centre will know, and we'll be Flagged, and I'll get an automatic fail. Even that's more than Mum would say. All she's done is try to get me ready for today. She's been giving me tablets with fish oil in them, omega something; I said they tasted funny and that I didn't want to take them. She shouted then, *really* shouted, about how I didn't know what she'd had to do to get them. I took them after that. Then Mum took me to the park a couple of times last week so that I could run. That was a waste of time though, it takes hours to get to the park and when you finally do, well, there's no room to do anything really, what with all the tents pitched everywhere. Mum says there used to be grass, but I don't see where.

I did try looking on the net for something about the Test, or the Centre. I couldn't find much really. It's not the same anymore anyway, not like it was before Google and Bing and all the rest were closed down last year. I did find one site—Fight the Test, it was called—but all that had on it were theories and guesswork about what happens, there wasn't anything concrete. I tried to go back there last week but they must have changed their address, cos I couldn't find it.

I had a look at the Centre's official site—that was mostly white too. It was funny though, they didn't have much on there either. When we've done tests at school, they've usually given us past questions to look at, and I was hoping they'd have the same on the Centre's site. But there was only one page, and that talked about the Test being "a matter of national importance" and "a way for every citizen to contribute towards the success and continuity of our great nation." Then there was the slogan, 'EARN YOUR PLACE!', in big red letters, followed by a very long list of all the Centres around the country.

I didn't like it when Mum and Dad dropped me off. Mum was all moist-eyed again, and I wondered if it was cos she was proud that I was going off to do my bit for the country, but she didn't look proud. She just looked sad. She was doing that thing where you chew your lip to stop yourself from crying. Then she gave me a hug and I had to tell her to get off cos the pavement outside the Centre was rammed, like it always is, and everyone could see and it was embarrassing. Dad slapped me on the shoulder. I said, 'See you later,' and Dad said, 'Do your best, son.' Mum didn't say anything. I moved forwards so that the Centre's entrance scanner could read me and the plain white, windowless door slid open. I stepped in and turned round to wave to Mum and Dad, but they were already being swept away in the crowd. That's the problem now that all the pavements are one-way, Dad reckons: makes it hard to stand still.

When the door closed behind me I wondered what to do, and whether the test was starting straight away but before I had chance to worry about anything else a man appeared from another door on the opposite side of the hall. He wore a long white coat that made me think of Dr Anderson, but he didn't look like a doctor. He didn't smile like Dr Anderson either, and he didn't have a badge or any pens in his top pocket. What he did have was a scanner like they have at school, and he swiped my code with that. Then he said Liam Bailey, 94738781?' and I said yes, cos he said it like a question which was funny cos he knew my name and number—he'd just scanned me. Then he said, 'Can you confirm that you were born on June 16th 2009?' and he must have known that too, but I said yes anyway. Dr Anderson would have said happy birthday or something, maybe 'You're a teenager now!' in his rumbly voice, but all this man said was, 'Follow me.'

We went through the doorway on the far side of the hall which led into a long corridor with no doors or windows. At least the carpet wasn't white. Walking along behind him, I noticed for the first time that the man had a mini-taser in his left hand, one of the ones that look like a pen. I recognised it straight away, cos it was the same make that all the teachers carry at school. Dad reckons he was tasered once, when he first met Mum. They were at some protest together and he reckons all he did was sit down in the road and a soldier shot him with a taser-net rifle. I asked what it had felt like and he said I couldn't imagine. Then I asked what they had been protesting about. He said it was for the Procreation Alliance, or Defiance, or something like that, but then Mum came running in from the kitchen and shouted at him to shut up, saying did he want to get us all Flagged? And that was the end of that. I asked him again a few days later, when Mum wasn't around, but all he'd say was, 'It was a long time ago.'

I was just starting to wonder how long this corridor was when it opened out into a small square room, all white of course. On one side was a desk that looked like it was stainless steel, like the bench I'm sat on now. The only other colour in the place was a single, large poster on the wall behind the desk that had the Centre's 'EARN YOUR PLACE!' slogan on in red letters.

A woman sat at the desk. She was wearing a white dress a bit like a nurse's and her hair was held back with a plain white ribbon. That *almost* made her look young, but her face was pale and waxy and old. I realised I was staring at her, and looked away quickly in case this was all part of the Test. Then she produced a scanner from a desk drawer, so I leaned my head forward so she could swipe my code. She said, 'Liam Bailey, 94738781?' just like the man had, and when I said yes she asked me to confirm my date of birth as well. She had a touch-PC on the desk in front of her, like the ones we used to have at school before they were taken away. Even upside down I could see my record on it. She tapped a button on the screen next to my photo and a progress bar appeared. Underneath, it said, 'Estimated time to completion: 44 minutes.'

Then she produced a clear plastic bag with a snap-top fastening and asked me to take off my watch and empty my pockets. I only had a couple of hundreds with me, and my phone, and the food coupon I'd been saving—they hardly seemed to fill the bag. Then she pulled out a metal tray and told me to take my shoes and belt off and put them in the tray. I thought this was starting to get a bit weird but didn't say so, I just did what I was told. Then she put the bag with my things in on top of the tray and the whole lot went back into her desk drawer.

While all this was going on, the man that had brought me in from the Centre's main entrance stood behind me, with his hands behind his back. He looked like one of the police that stand outside school, except without the face mask.

I was just getting up the courage to ask when the Test started, when the woman behind the desk said, 'Take a seat in the waiting room please,' and pointed at a plain white door opposite her. She pressed something under her desk and the door slid open. The man stood aside and I went in, and that's where I am now.

It's hard to judge how long I've been sat in here, without a watch and everything, but it's got be to well over half an hour now, easily. There are two light-boxes on the ceiling, one either side of a fine metal grill, and one of the boxes is humming. The light-box in my bedroom used to hum like that too, when I was little. One night, when Mum had come up to tuck me in, she said that the humming reminded her of b's. I asked her what b's were but she just sighed, kissed me goodnight and went downstairs. When I got home from school the next day, the light-box was gone.

I've been sat here all this time and the only thing that has happened is the smell has changed. Just in the last minute or so, there's been a faint sweet smell coming from somewhere—it reminds me of the sugarex we used to have, before food coupons. It's making me feel hungry—breakfast seems ages ago. Mum got me up early today, to make sure I'd be ready for the Test, so maybe that's why I feel so tired now. That and the buzzing light-box, maybe. I can hardly keep my eyes open. It won't hurt if I just lie down for a bit, will it, just put my feet up on the bench and close my eyes for a few minutes, have a nap. I'm sure that nurse woman will call me when it's time to take the Test, and this way I'll be properly rested for it.

Now my eyes are closed, all I can sense is the light-box hum and the sugarex smell, which is definitely getting stronger, I can almost taste it now. My tummy's rumbling—maybe I'll spend my food coupon after the Test. Right now though, so tired…just a nap, a little one…it won't hurt, will it?

The Mall

- Deborah Arnander -

I saw your mum today. After thirteen years, I'm surprised I recognised her, but I did. She's working at the church next to the mall; I think she's serving coffee there. At any rate, she was taking in the board. And I was walking through the graveyard, on my way to the shops, when she looked up, with a frown on her face. For a second, our eyes met. I couldn't move. She looked me in the eye so searchingly that I imagined something floating there, curled over like a comma in the green part of my eye. But then her mouth shut in a disappointed line, as if her hope had made her sad, and there was nothing left alive in me at all. She turned away, still carrying her board, and I walked on. As I walked I realised that she'd been searching there for you. I didn't turn back then. My heart was pounding and I couldn't catch my breath. I thought: at least I didn't smile. Not after last time. She might have run at me and ripped the hair out of my head. She might have kicked me to the floor and stamped on me. And I wouldn't have fought back. I'll tell you now, Rhia: if I could make it up to you, I would.

I'm glad the grass is growing back, in that churchyard. When they built the path, to provide access to the mall, they took the headstones up, then rolled and raked the earth. So for a while the soil beside the path was loose. Every time I went through there, on my lunch break, I would picture a hand, its nails packed with dirt, and then an arm, and then a hundred other hands, uncurling like seeds. At first the headstones were stacked up against the wall, but now they have been planted in the bright green turf. Only the old and pretty ones, of course. There was a rumour that a workman found a bunch of skulls, which he sold round the pubs. It must have made your mother mad, to see that soil disturbed. It's not as if you're buried there, I know. I also know that it reminded me.

So I walked on through the plaza, glancing at the wedding shop (a dark model wore a red velvet cloak, with fur around the hood) and then at Office (slouchy 80s boots, in mustard, green and airforce blue), and all the while I thought about your mother in her church. I've never been inside it: churches still give me the creeps. From outside, the church is squat and grey, the colour of a cold day at the beach, and you look past it to the swooping steel and glass and halogen that sparkles like clear sunlight in the mall. People with their bags are always passing by; I suppose they hoped—the church people, like your mum—that some of those shoppers would come in. I've read the board, their tea and coffee's cheap: not half the price of Starbucks'. You don't know about Starbucks. I'll take you there. You'll like it: there are different kinds of cakes, and everywhere this sweet, vanilla smell, like baby's breath. Anyway, I think your mother was alone. Did she start praying, after she saw me? Weeping? Planning her revenge? We'll have to ask her. She won't mind telling you.

I passed through the entrance to the mall, under the giant TV screen—forecasting a blustery day, with wind speeds up to forty miles an hour—and joined the other shoppers with their winter faces, their hushed shuffling. I was reminded of your funeral. I remembered, in the quiet bit, for prayers, the squelch of noses being blown: and I remembered myself, giggling. It echoed from the rafters like a high-pitched neigh, all the more shrill for being suppressed. I didn't mind at first. Most of my friends were trying not to smile—because everyone was nervous, naturally. It was me your mother noticed: I was the one who couldn't stop. I held my breath, to keep the laughter down, but when I breathed again, I could not reach the air. It was like sucking through a leaky straw. Mrs Daniel had to take me out. As I crouched panting on the gravel I could see the pit for your coffin from the corner of my eye. There was a pile of damp sand beside it, and a green tarpaulin with a pool of water in the middle, because the night before the service it had rained. The edges were held down with bricks; any more weight and those bricks would start to slide. When the service was over, we gathered around the hole, uncovered now, and deep. Your mother's face was red and creased with tears, and the box swayed as it was lowered in on ropes, its black wood clean as polished shoes against the walls of mud. A bird was singing, clear hard notes like drops of glass. Your mum leaned out, to let the dirt fall from her hand, and looked as though she might follow you in.

Back in the mall I felt that panic flutter start to rise, and counted in my head to slow my breath. They'd changed the store displays, for Christmas time. Red pictures in the windows of the gallery: so many things, this time of year, seem to be drenched in blood. Or drained of it: in Esprit, the dummies in their festive gear were stony white, and had been guillotined; I wondered if their heads were in those big handbags of theirs. I ducked into Zara. I thought, to take my mind off it, I'd try on party clothes.

They had the usual winter colours in: damsons, charcoal greys, and blacks, and chiffon gowns with sparkles on. I was fingering materials and pulling hangers to and fro, and again I thought of you. I thought, I could have helped you look your best. There are clothes for every figure: even yours. Do you remember that time when we were in the science lab? You turned round on your stool because you heard us, me and Isobel: we were behind you, measuring your arse. It was wider than the ruler, easily. We worked out you had forty-inch hips. And you were just fourteen! But today I thought: something like this, an Empire line, falling from a seam below the bust. In a grown-up colour: a peaty sort of brown. You'd have to dye your hair, of course. You can get serums now that would sort out the frizz; you could even straighten it, but not too lank, because with cheeks like yours, you need a bit of volume in your hair.

I took a couple of dresses: one in chiffon paisley with big black sequins on—I'd wear it with gold jewellery, midnight Russian style—and the other, peaty one, that I'd thought of for you. I didn't have to wait; there are lots of changing rooms at Zara, with mirrors you can adjust the angle of, to get an all-round view. I tried the chiffon dress; my arms aren't what they were, but I didn't dwell on that: with a silk polo underneath, I thought, it will be fine. Then I tried the brown. It had a couple of buttons, high up at the back; I lowered my head to reach around and fasten them. When I looked up, in the mirror, you were there.

It was your posture that I noticed first: the sagging shoulders, sloping to your neck. When you were a teenager, your boobs just cried out for a better bra. And there was a smell, a scurfy kind of smell, like you get on your fingers when you've scratched your head. It's not my smell: I shower every day, and wash and dry my hair. I looked at my face—what should have been my face—and there were your round eyes, the eye-rims pink and sore, the lashes sparse, the irises a weak, diluted blue. Their expression was your usual one, of mild, hopeless surprise. The same one that you had the day you saw me shoplifting. Or that other time, when you caught me with Anton, being Martini girl at school. And something happened. I looked at you and thought, I should be horrified, but it could not come through. It was like I had a slower pulse, and thicker blood, which took a longer time to flow, and as it flowed, unhurriedly, it carried something from you through my veins, like a pre-med, that dulled things down, and shut them out, as though Helen, the old Helen, were just a screaming child, locked in a room, in a big house, and I was busy somewhere, out of earshot, far away.

From the mirror, you smiled. It was the same smile you gave me, the first time we ever met, when I sat by you in Miss Stirling's class. It's an accepting smile; there are no sideways looks to check my shoes, see what my pencil case is like. You haven't changed: you're older now, you've grown a bit—not fatter though, thank God. You never did change, did you? When all of us hit puberty and started trying different faces on, you were still potato head, with added spots. Your mum was strict, of course, but I don't think you cared. You didn't want to do the things that we did, anyway.

Any time, any place, anywhere… That used to be my name, Martini girl. I had no shame about it, not at first, not till it all turned nasty, as it was bound to do. But standing in that changing room in Zara, earlier today, I saw it through your eyes. I'm walking in on me and Anton in the girl's cloakroom, and my mouth drops and I feel my stomach shrink, because from where I'm standing now it looks as though he's hurting me.

When I was the new girl and you were my only friend, I once went home to tea with you. We were twelve years old. You opened the door, and ran to find your mother in the kitchen. I can see the wallpaper, in your hall: off-white, with a pattern of floating olive leaves, like teeming fish; I hung back there, watching. When you reached your mother, she held out her arm, and caught you in it, and she curled her hand around and laid it on your brow. You nestled in to her, and closed your eyes. I didn't know what to do with myself. I felt lonely, and furious.

Nobody guessed that you would go so far. You didn't plan to suffer, which is good. If they had left you, under your duvet, in your bed, you wouldn't have; as it was, you hung on for a week. You were too sick for visitors. The whole class—nearly the whole class—all went, together, to your funeral; Mrs Daniel drove us in the minibus. It would never happen now, not at a school today. And what we did to you: you know it wasn't my idea, although I shouldn't have told Isobel, about your face when you saw me with Anton, and the stupid things you said. Isobel said that it was time you learned: nobody should be so innocent. Then you just lay there, on the floor, and let Anton, and afterwards he claimed that we had used him too. I wish I could forget the look you gave me, over his shoulder, or afterwards, the nervous way you wiped your mouth, your knock-kneed walk along the corridor; your skirt was creased, and, where you'd sat down on it, stained. We weren't even late for Geography, though Mr Parfitt had to send you out, because you just stared and wouldn't answer him.

So we'll put on the brown dress, and I will do your hair, and we'll go and see your mother, in her church beside the mall. When she looks in my eyes, I know she'll find you there. I'm hoping she'll stretch out her arm, and pull me close to her. She'll rest her hand upon my brow, and bless us both this time.

The Last Dog and Pony Show

- Sherilyn Connelly -

The Dog and Pony Show was a few days away. It was the biggest animal role-playing event of the year, and my girlfriend Vash wanted me there to see her as a pony. Even though her other lover and primary pony trainer Dietrich wasn't going to attend, the event didn't feel safe. But it was a rare and wonderful thing when Vash wanted me around these days, so I couldn't say no.

I asked her what I would do at The Dog and Pony Show, and Vash replied: 'You can be one of the humans who grooms me and feeds me carrots.'

I winced. No. No, no, no. That was so *distant*. I needed to be more involved, to be on her level, to *participate*, not to just be another anonymous visitor at the petting zoo.

All the same, a million questions went through my mind, and most of them came out of my mouth: 'What kind of carrots?' 'Pre-packaged baby carrots, or regular ones cut into chunks?' 'How often?' 'How close can I get?' 'Will there be, like, a pen or something?' 'Will it cost extra for me as a human?' 'And what should I wear?' And and and...

Vash's reply to each question was: 'I don't know, Sherilyn. I've never gone before.'

She spoke in plain English and without metaphor, yet I didn't grasp her point: *this was new for her.* Not just The Dog and Pony Show, but being a pony in public. According to my infallible imagination, she'd been doing nothing but pony play with Dietrich for the last six months, both at Vash's house (on her bed, or in that comfy chair I liked) and amongst Dietrich's friends, all of whom envied Dietrich for scoring as wonderful a ponygirl as Vash. I needed to prove my worthiness as an animal play partner, or even just as Vash's primary partner beyond my current vestigial status. I was sure she already had the whole weekend mapped out. I just wanted to know where I fit in, if I fit in at all.

After another barrage of questions from me, Vash—the oldest of three children, an inverse to how I was born the youngest of four—said: 'Do you know what you're doing, Sherilyn? You're acting like you have Little Sister Syndrome. That's when the big sister discovers something new, and the little sister is all "Oooh! Oooh! What is that? I wanna do it too!"'

I flashed on all the times I'd wanted to join my older brothers in whatever they were doing, but they didn't want the baby of the family around. It hadn't happened for decades, but…ouch. And I knew Vash wasn't wrong, either.

I said: 'I'm sorry. Look, I just won't go. It doesn't feel right.'

Sounding somewhat reluctant, Vash said: 'Well, maybe you can be a pony.'

I brightened. This was what I'd been hoping she would say, the invitation I'd been waiting for months to hear. And it was imminent, the end of this week, less liable to fall through the cracks like so many other things we were going to do together. (I'd long since accepted that we would never make it to New York together, let alone fuck on the Staten Island Ferry, a plan we'd made during the heady early days of our relationship.)

The two obvious practical issues were that I had no experience as a pony—however little Vash may have had, I still had less—and that I would need a trainer. Vash said her friend Abby was already going to have her hands full with Vash. I wasn't sure why Abby couldn't handle both Vash *and* me, being the advanced pony-handler that she was, but if Vash said it wasn't an option, it wasn't an option. I would have to be an animal which wouldn't require a trainer, one which by its nature was solitary…

…like a cat! Of course! Though I never admitted it to the pony-obsessed Vash for fear of further alienating her from me, I was indifferent to all things equestrian. Maybe it was because I was born and socialized male, not coming out as transsexual and transitioning to female until my mid-twenties, so I missed out on whatever elements of the female childhood so often result in the horse fixation. However, I'm a cat person in the classic sense of the word. I love cats and they love me. Vash's nickname for me was even Gatocita, *faux*-Spanish for 'little cat.' So, yes. I'd be a cat.

I started asked her questions again, this time about being a cat. Vash grew silent.

According to urban legend, the Inuit have identified dozens of different kinds of snow. I was developing a similar catalog for different kinds of silence. This silence meant Vash didn't want to say anything which might be taken the wrong way. Or, worse, the right way. It translated as: *stop. just stop before I change my mind about the whole thing.* So I did.

The Dog and Pony was show being held at The Power Exchange, the most controversial sex club in town. Vash and I arrived early that afternoon for the orientation classes, which were long but informative. The gist was that when someone was in animal mode, you treat them as that animal. That made perfect sense to me, because as a transsexual it's what I ask of the world on a daily basis. *um, hi. here's my deal: i identify and (hopefully) present as female, so i'd appreciate it you'd treat me as female. plzkthxbai!*

The concept of the totem animal was discussed—the specific animal the person feels closest toward, an affinity for, what they have inside them. Mine, of course, was a cat. Nothing else came close. I considered declaring it to be a pony in order to feel closer to Vash—*see? see how much we still have in common? play with me, too!*—but that would be dishonest. I was a cat. Besides, ponies were discouraged from being alone, so I'd need a human. And I didn't have a human. Even as a human, I didn't really have a human.

I wasn't the least bit surprised to learn that animal play tended to focus on dogs and ponies—hence the name of the event, itself a term which had been around for over a century. Though welcome, cats fell into the broader category of 'other'. I had to laugh. Of *course* cats were other. It was the story of my life: even when I was welcome, here in the midst of the kinkiest of the kinky, I was still an alien.

Much of animal play, we were told, is about 'being in touch with your body.' I found myself wondering how that could be a good thing. (*Other* bodies, sure, OK. Like Vash's. But not mine.) For some people it's all about the BDSM aspect, about being topped and controlled and owned, and for some it isn't. It varied from person to person, as all things must. I liked the idea of being an animal bottom, having someone else in control, and most importantly, being loved and cared for, the way I loved and cared for my cat Perdita.

The furry presentation was given by a furry named Smash. Smash the Furry! Wearing a red-and-white PVC fox costume, he talked about the overlap between animal role-players and furries, their similarities and differences. The line was blurry, but some people defended it, much like how I defended the line between transvestite and transsexual. To the general public it all looked the same: animal role-player equaled furry, and transsexual equaled transvestite. If you weren't one of those groups, the differences between them were hairs that were not worth splitting.

Even though it's often found in sexually charged atmospheres such as The Power Exchange, animal role-play tends to be rather chaste, focusing more on fantasy and make-believe than anything sexual. The animal may get petted, referred to as getting scritches, but for all intents and purposes the bestiality taboo remained intact.

On the other hand, furries often had a strong sex and/or BDSM proclivity, since the imaginary species lines being crossed didn't involve humans. Known as 'yiffing,' sex in the furry community was everywhere, but not discussed in public. The American conservative streak popped up in the strangest places, and I wasn't surprised to discover it deep within a marginalized fetish.

The next class was taught by Pixie the Pony, a small red-haired woman. She was a switch, sometimes a pony and sometimes a human. At the moment, she was in full trainer gear, and to me her class was the most important: getting into the animal headspace through meditation.

Vash and I had been sitting together all day long. Before the class began she got up to use the restroom. When she was done, she sat down in the first spot she could find, on the far side of the room from me. This was practical, understandable and reasonable.

It was also painful. I couldn't concentrate, and I couldn't hear Pixie speaking. I couldn't hear anything at all over the sound of my heart breaking.

I told myself it was a lesson, a reminder of what I always knew: *i am alone. there is only me. i am here without her, just as i would be if she sat back down next to me.*

Focus, focus, focus. I'd been reading Pema Chodron's *When Things Fall Apart*, because heaven knew things were falling apart right now, and I tried to do what it suggested: *use the loneliness, embrace it, embrace the fear, this is about me not her*—

Pixie began the meditation. It was what I was there to do, it was what I was going to do, and that was that. Much like those nights I'd spent here at The Power Exchange to distract myself from the thought of Vash with Dietrich, what anyone else was or was not doing was none of my concern, even if they were on the other side of the room

'Lie down. Close your eyes. Think of the animal, picture it—the physicality, the breed.' I thought of Perdita. I'd had her for two years now, since breaking up with Maddy, and she was now my role model. Everything I needed to know to be a cat, I learned from her.

Pixie told us to slowly move into the sleeping animal's position. I rolled from my back onto my side and approximated the way Perdita slept next to me, my arms and legs in front of me and crossed.

'Now, wake up slowly. Don't rush it. Wake up as the animal, and explore the world around you.'

I opened my eyes and slowly propped myself up. The others were doing the same. I imagined how weirded out Perdita would feel right now, and realized I was feeling it, too. It was spooky to be around these other awakening animals. At the same time, being down there felt natural.

I began moving around on my hands and knees, keeping my distance from the others yet curious about them. A large dog with a spiked collar growled at me, and I shrank back, hissing. In another direction, a bunny regarded me, unsure. (I knew she was bunny because she'd told me earlier in the day.) A smaller dog approached me and licked my paw. She wanted to be friends, I could tell. Not like that other dog. That other dog scared me.

Pixie told us to lie back down. I returned to my Perdita-sleep position, and we stayed there for a few minutes. I wondered if I was dreaming.

Finally I twitched and stretched and awakened, back to human.

Wow. I liked that. *A lot.* And I did it alone, as I always was.

The ponies and domestic dogs were told to stay upstairs, and the rest of us—the Others, the ones who didn't even fit in with the misfits—were sent downstairs to the Dungeon. We had a classic around-the-circle discussion of what animal we were, what breed and so on. Among them were a wolf, the bunny, a dragon (!), as well as Smash the Furry, who had changed out of the fox costume and into what I supposed was a more traditional furry outfit, resembling comfy-looking pajamas with hoodie and ears.

There was a twenty year-old boy who identified as a deer. He made no bones about wanting to be a hardcore furry, and looked at Smash with open admiration. It was quite touching, and I respected him for being so unapologetic about his desires and true to his own wiring.

I mean, he *had* to know that being a furry was an invitation to scorn and ridicule, and if he hadn't known it before, Smash covered the topic in his presentation earlier. But the kid didn't care, or at least wasn't going to let that stop him. I could relate, since I made a similar leap of faith when I came out as transsexual. The big difference was furry culture had only become common knowledge over the past decade or thanks to the internet, as people sat at their computers and laughed at fetishists who at least were getting out in the world, and furries were the biggest laughingstock. Meanwhile, I grew up seeing transvestites and transsexuals played as cheap punchlines on sitcoms, or pathetic, tragic figures on dramas and talk shows, or sources of homosexual panic (and often outright killers) in movies. I reflected on all the little future furries out there, perhaps too young to express it beyond knowing what they wanted to dress up as for Halloween, who would first see furries in a similar context of scorn and mockery yet think to themselves: *hey, that's me! That's what I wanna do!*

For all the exoticism of the other animals—Vash herself was even a specialized breed of pony—I knew I was just a garden variety housecat, a dime a dozen. Not a kitten, either. I'd always thought kittens were overrated. I was an adult cat, and all I knew of my breed was that I wasn't a tabby. If anything, I had long black hair like Perdita. But there was nothing special about me, just another lone feline.

We were asked to think of what elements of our personality were shared by the animal in question, if any at all. A description popped into my head: *attention-starved yet aloof, slutty yet finicky, skittish, fiercely loyal yet ultimately alone.* Yeah, sounded like Perdita. Sounded like me.

Back upstairs, I chatted with Smash (who I was not at all surprised to discover was a Linux geek) about *Star Trek* and other nerdy matters. He also told me I reminded him of a girl he'd dated in the nineties. She had the same look and style, so much so that when I first walked in he thought I was her. It was a dumb coincidence, but I found it flattering all the same. It's always a compliment to be parsed as a genetic female. It means I'm doing something right.

That evening over dinner, I barraged Vash with questions again. 'So...will we talk to each other? I mean, I know animals don't talk, but maybe it can be like in movies where they talk to each other but not to humans? Because it seems to me that animals would have a common dialect, a 'pidgin' if you want to get strictly linguistic about it, and I think we should in this case, one that transcends species, and—'

Vash was looking at me impassively. 'Sherilyn, you're doing it again.'

Realizing the answer a moment too late, I asked: 'Doing what?…oh! Oh. Right. Little Sister Syndrome. OK. You're right. Sorry.' It hurt, but I couldn't deny it at this point, either. I *was* the tag-along, the outsider. The Little Sister.

But I was in it for the long haul, and I wasn't backing out. I just wouldn't ask any more questions. Much like answering truthfully, asking questions only ever got me into trouble. I would just *be*, watch, observe, lurk. And when nobody was looking, participate in the margins.

We went to Abby's house to get ready. Abby focused on getting Vash together, so I was left up to my own devices. It helped that my costume consisted of my street clothes plus a pair of kitty ears and a tail.

Listening to Abby and Vash talk in the other room, I learned that Vash's pony name—which had been Darling One when she was playing with Dietrich—was now Pepper.

Nobody asked, but my cat name was Ezri.

The Dog and Pony Show was in full swing when we arrived at The Power Exchange. Finding a quiet place to meditate as Pixie recommended was not an option, so, into the breach: I got down on all fours, and stopped speaking English. Going sub-verbal, they called it. Meows and hisses and purrs and other such sounds. It was like a switch was flipped.

CAT: not human

There are other animals everywhere, barking and meowing and neighing in languages I don't recognize. Sometimes an animal howls, and the rest of us harmonize in a beautiful, bestial echo.

Abby leads Pepper towards the ring, a section cordoned off with a rope fence. Cats don't herd, but they do often follow if they want to. And Ezri wants to follow the pony.

She's very fond of Pepper. Does Pepper know it? Could she return it if she did?

Ezri doesn't know, and though Ezri is sometimes brave she's also skittish by nature. She doesn't get too close to Pepper. If she goes too far into where she doesn't belong, she might get yelled at, and that hurts.

We pass by dogs—Spike! That's Spike, I remember him from earlier, he seems nice—and the large predatory dog, now with white pupils and large spiked collar, leashed and restrained, growling and hungry. I hiss as I pass, to let him know that I'm not afraid. He snarls back.

When people were in our way, I keep going, around or more often through their legs. Pepper is standing upright, as ponies will.

And there was Smash the Furry in his Leatherwolf outfit. Looked expensive. More than my ears, that's for sure.

The Parade of Pets begins. In keeping with the faux-egalitarian ideals of this upper echelon of San Francisco sex culture, it is an exhibition, not a competition. There is no wagering, and there are no awards or ribbons. In anticipation of this, Vash made ribbons for Abby and Pepper, for Best Trainer and Best Pony.

Ezri doesn't get a ribbon. Cats don't get ribbons.

Other animals are announced and paraded, and finally us. I can't tell for sure, I can't see in the ring well and there are so many other sounds and sights to take in, but I don't think anyone else brings cats into the Parade.

I was there because Abby had called for me to follow her, and with everything else going on she was still my human, but otherwise, I'm not sure what we're doing, why all the people are looking at us. It seems to have something to do with Pepper, but I don't know what. People always make a big fuss about her.

There are other cats when we exit, new and different cats, some I recognize from other bodies and some not. We're tactile, rubbing up against each other and nuzzling and licking whether we know each other or not, and it's nice.

Humans sometimes feed us by hand. Pez and other small things. Scritches on the head as we chew.

I talk a lot. Only cat, never human. My human brain thinks of jokes, always running like it is, and sometimes I meow in appropriate tones— *mrrowr? mrrowr mrrowr, mrrowr. mrrowr!*—but I couldn't speak human.

Abby is carrying a basket, and she places it on the ground, saying she hopes the kitty will watch it. Ezri watches the basket for a few moments before she realizes she doesn't really understand human, certainly nothing as complex as whatever Abby just said, and with so much external stimuli she can't pick up on *everything*…

…and Abby and Pepper are gone now. No, no, Ezri can't be left alone, not here, not now…

I chase after them, crying (*mrrowr? mrrowr!*). Since the Parade is over, Abby has taken Pepper into the ring to run and jump. Ezri goes up to the fence and watches from a respectful distance.

Abby sees me watching and invites me in. Yay! I scramble through the fence and go to Pepper's side. I nuzzle against her, meow, and back away. A little is enough.

When Pepper rests, Ezri nuzzles her leg. Pepper leans over and places her hooves on Ezri's back. Ezri knows Pepper's horseshoes are a gift from Dietrich, engraved with Pepper's old name DARLING ONE, but that's OK. It still feels wonderful. Does this mean that Pepper likes her, Ezri wonders, or is she just a place for Pepper to put her hooves? Is this the sign? Ezri isn't sure she can trust it. She doesn't want to be wrong and get in trouble.

Abby tells Ezri she's taking Pepper downstairs. Oh. OK. Ezri's heart sinks a little. So that's that.

Abby then says: 'Would the kitty like to come along?'

Oh yes yes yes thank you mom…

Other than a 'critter theme' to acknowledge the quasi-bestial madness happening upstairs, it's a typical Saturday night in the Dungeon. It's all damned spooky to Ezri, humans doing scary things to each other.

They stop at an empty table. Abby moves a chair in front of it and tells Ezri to get up. Ezri lumbers onto the table.

She watches as Abby brushes Pepper, her mane, her hooves, all over. Then Abby massages Ezri's paws, which feels wonderful. Abby tells Pepper what a great kitty Ezri is, how surprised she is, that Ezri's better than most new kitties. *Yay! thanks, mom!*

Abby says she's going upstairs for a few minutes, and for the pony and cat to wait here for her. OK.

Pixie the Pony is lead over by her trainer, attracted by Ezri's meowing. Ezri leans forward, and they sniff each other. Pixie snorts, Ezri mews. Pixie's different from Pepper, somehow. Does she want to be friends? Ezri reaches out her paw. This spooks Pixie. She backs up, and her trainer leads her away. Ezri is confused. What did she do wrong?

Ezri's still on the table, and Pepper is standing next to it. Pepper nudges Ezri back a little, then climbs onto the table. There's more than enough room for them both.

Pepper moves in even closer, and they nuzzle. Pepper looks into Ezri's eyes and smiles. It's like a glow on the Eastern horizon at the end of a long autumn night. Pepper kisses Ezri, and both my cat and human hearts feel like they're going to burst. (Ezri: *she loves me and wants me around!* Sherilyn: *she still loves me and wants me around!*) The pain and uncertainty of recent months fades away.

Abby returns, nonplussed that Pepper is on the table with Ezri. She leads Pepper and Ezri back upstairs to the ring, and runs Pepper in laps.

I slink away and make myself comfortable. It's been an exhausting night. I watch Pepper and Abby do their final laps and jumps for the evening. When they're done, Abby brings Pepper over. I nuzzle Pepper's legs. Pepper leans over and rests her horseshoes on Ezri's back, Ezri purring and meowing, constantly. Like the kiss downstairs, this is the closeness I'd been craving, what I'd been hoping to find when I crossed over.

Abby says it's getting to be about time to call it a night. Pepper agrees, but Ezri is not so sure. She doesn't want to go away, not yet. The problem with immersion is that when it ends, it gets taken away and never comes back.

Vash returned home with me that night. As she curled up next to me in bed and fell asleep, I felt more hopeful than I'd been in months.

We were going to make it.

Extract from The Lemonade Girl

- Sarah Dobbs -

My wife knew my missing-presumed-dead ex girlfriend was back before I did, right before I got the letter.

'You've got that look, Michael.'

Karen was naked when she said this, in the bed where we made our two young children, the darkness a cloak to all the detritus that we ought to have tidied away, a darkness pricked only by the lemony glow of my reading lamp. Karen was on her right side, turned towards me, hands pressed together under her head as though in prayer. I could smell the coconut body milk she's used since I bought her a set on our first anniversary. I don't think she likes it; it's a concession to me. In reality, I picked it up last minute at The Body Shop in Euston after a conference.

'What look?' I flipped the page without taking in the print. First year work; paying close attention was not strictly necessary.

Karen's hands were tucked under her head, the white-blonde hair that picks her out of any room foams over the organza silk pillow, falling into the creases. Her lips displayed the sulk that first attracted me to her. Not that she's moody, far from it; it was more of a sexy pout than anything else. A look that said, I'm thinking of you naked. The sheer availability of Karen's emotions appealed to me. I could always read her, always know what she was thinking. Her life had been one of absolute, untainted ordinariness. At the time, that was exactly what I needed. Nothing complicated.

'It's the look that says you're leaving me again, that you're already gone. You're writing about your ex again, aren't you?'

Oh here we go. My shoulders sagged and I put the work on the bedside table to my right, balancing it on top of the wide, flat alarm that looked like an oversized pill. It sieved off and into a heap on the floor.

'Fuck.'

'Leave it will you, Michael? Come on. Talk to me?'

I hooked my glasses off with one finger and set them down on the table. 'About what?'

'You know what. After all this time, why can't you let go of Beth-Anne? Aren't me and the kids enough for you?'

How can I answer that honestly? Sorry, Karen, I love you but you'll just never quite measure up. I chose my words carefully. She can't know the whole truth. Her frame of reference does not equip her to handle this knowledge. I reminded myself that this was part of why I loved Karen. It would not do to mention how I was beginning to wonder whether Beth-Anne, the girl who'd haunted me since I was a lanky twenty four year old, all immersed in the passion of the Romantic period and just going in for my viva, was, after all, not actually dead. Worse still would be if I mentioned that I was thinking of trying to track my ex girlfriend down. Wrong. That I'd already starting looking. That I had to know.

'Don't talk soft, Karen, course you're enough. The three of you are my life, you know that. Come here.'

Karen's body was supple; her breasts were still, in the main, full and the slope of her stomach felt warm under my palm. Her skin creased near her bellybutton. I thought of week-old peaches and got a jolt of warmth and familiarity. Karen was *home*. And yet lately, the only way I could have sex with my wife was by imagining the girl that came before her, the one who'll never leave me. I ran my hand over the peach-skin. It whispered, the friction of skin against skin. In my mind, I thought of my wife's skin as just tracing paper, placed over the girl I used to touch, that I am drawing Beth-Anne's outline by touch and memory alone.

With effort, forcing Beth-Anne to the back of my mind, I embarked on that slow clamber, the sequence that turns my wife onto her back, her legs parting, giving up to me. The kiss on the nose, eyelid, chin, neck, breastbone; I smelled coconut, the body milk sour on my tongue, her right nipple puckering like a knot held fast in my lips. And to enter my wife, I thought of my dick bursting through that tracing paper, and reaching a place that, no matter how much I desired it, I could never return to.

I dream about a car crash, a bad one. There's a chameleon on the dash, watching, shutters blinking over sideways eyes. Everyone dies except me. Karen and the kids were all dead in a wrench and knot of metal. I killed them. Me. Because I'd been preoccupied after receiving a token off Beth-Anne–*proof.* I go careering off some South American cliff into dizzyingly clear blue sky. We crash. I'm deafened and stiffened by the brace of water. My family's voices are just bubbles in the murk.

I woke with everything still and deep-dark. I prickled with sweat, an actual ache in my chest. Shit. I groaned like it was Monday and Karen draped her leg over my torso. But who was I mourning? My family, or Beth-Anne?

The next morning, it was all toast and Cornflakes and Karen shaping tin foil tight over cheese and tomato sandwiches—she won't use plastic bags, she told me why once—clicking pink and blue lunchboxes closed. Their background noise was warm; I wanted this with Beth-Anne, now I have it with Karen. That should be enough.

'Daddy?'

I gulped down black coffee and scribbled 'supporting ref?!' onto one of the assignments I should have finished last night.

Karen picked up for me, like I knew she would. 'Daddy's working Mia. What's wrong?'

'David says we don't love him as much because his name begins with D and not M and D is a bad grade.'

I looked at David over the top of my glasses and the assignment (definite lower 2:2, if only because this student was far too cocky). David was the quiet one, darker haired but still sandy; the analyser. Mia pushed her specs up with one finger and reset the heart-shaped clip in her white-blonde hair, kicking her heels against the breakfast stool looking, as always, at David. Her eyes were huge behind her glasses. She's got Retinitis Pigmentosa; it made her ice-blue eyes startlingly beautiful. She'd be totally blind by the time she's forty. I hated the fact that I loved her more for this flaw, maybe more than David.

Is my damaged daughter my fault, my punishment? Karen had held my head, fast and stern, against her breasts one night when I said this shortly after Mia was diagnosed. She'd stroked my hair until I fell asleep as though dragging out the poisons in my brain through sheer will.

'Mia, eat your cereal. David, don't be silly. David means 'beloved' in Hebrew.'

David shrugged. 'Never said it anyway.'

'The milk tastes fucky, Mummy.'

Karen and I looked at each other, our faces relaxing at the same time. 'Funky,' Karen says. 'You mean funky, honey.'

'Fucky. S'what I said, Mummy.'

David ate slowly, having trimmed his toast of crusts. He was arranging them in a mix of horizontal and vertical lines, like Tetris. The pattern reminded me of something I couldn't quite grasp. He looked tired. I knew I should say something, but couldn't think what. He didn't get picked for football, and I didn't know where to begin on his one obsession: medicine. Some day very soon, my son would be cleverer than me. It made me nervous.

Mia started complaining about the fact that David got the last model out of the Cornflakes box so why should he get the new one too?

'Because cars are boys' toys, OK?'

'But David doesn't even eat cereal.'

'Full of sugars,' he mumbled.

David talked so quietly, compared to Mia's bell-like voice, that it was arresting. I watched him, flicking back and forth from the next to last paper which described Coleridge's *Ancient Mariner* as a 'twit who is doomed to hell for obviously not being vegetarian, or an animal lover, which is advanced thinking for them days because people didn't know about vegetarians then'. I drew a line down the whole page that discussed this and wrote 'Irrelevant, relate to question.' David's jaw slowly ground down his toast.

'Teethy-pegs, kids.' Karen stood still for a moment and squeezed my shoulder. Her hand was hot through my shirt. 'Come on, time to brush.'

I was still looking at David when he straightened like a dog that's heard an intruder and was about to embark on full-scale howling.

'Dad. Someone's at the door. *Dad.*'

Mia was still chunnering on about the unfairness of the Cornflakes toy and how if women could drive cars then little girls could play with them, because Mummy drives a car.

My eyes still on David, my gut starting that I-might-need-a-shit-soon churn, I chipped in with, 'Mummy drive? Debatable, My-Oh-Mia.'

Karen thwacked me with the back of her hand and called 'Teethy-pegs' for the second time. There was a knock at the door. David looked at me but Karen went to answer it. The both of us, David and I, or so it seemed to me, were on pause. The world swirled around us, and we waited. Mia whirled her arm around inside the Cornflake box, hunting.

'Who was it?'

'Huh? Oh nothing, love, just the post.'

'But there was a knock.'

Karen looked at me, sorting through the envelopes. She shook her head. 'Post. One for you.'

'It's a love letter off Mummy,' Mia said. She made kissing noises.

I looked sharply at Mia who frowned, about to cry. And then she did. Karen widened her eyes at me; I shrugged.

David watched me as I opened the letter. The envelope was small, about the size of a strip of aspirin, cool in my palm. I checked the postmark; it was smudged and unreadable. The lip of the envelope gave and the gum was faded Sellotape-yellow. It was the paper that struck me. Tracing paper, Bible-page-thin. I tucked the envelope in my jacket pocket.

'What was it, Michael? A lurve letter?' Karen flicked her eyebrows.

I wrinkled my nose. 'Nothing. Moaning letter from a student. Better be off.'

I kissed my wife and my little girl, felt like a prick for only waving at David, grabbed my briefcase and went. When I got in the car, I couldn't fucking breathe. My fingers were jittery, like the students' when they're asked to read work aloud. I knew without reading it that the letter was, had to be, from Beth-Anne.

It was only later when I was indicating off onto the slip road towards the university, maybe jolted by the white hatched lines, that I was reminded of David's toast-Tetris. It hadn't occurred to me at the time, but now, I'm sure he was recreating a skeleton.

*

'Fucking door.' I jiggled my office key. I wanted to disappear before Brad Keene could get the boot in. I could smell the guy loping down the other end of the corridor towards me, all buttered up in a vat of Calvin Klein aftershave. I'm reminded of that character in Charlie Brown, the one whose dirt swirled about him.

'Mornin' Michael,' Brad said.

Brad Keene was a total jock-strapped faux-academic from LA. He wrote shit poetry about gay sex despite the fact he was straighter than a fucking ruler. Apparently, that's transgressive. But then that actor with the jaw read one out on Graham Norton and they sold a shit load. So they made Brad a professor. The guy'd never submitted anything for the Research Assessment Exercise in his life, but happily continued writing about shitting cum. The secretaries reckon he was fucking one of the undergrads. Some opinionated eighteen-year old Greek girl with hair like black candyfloss. I was a little jealous. Her vowels came out of her mouth, full, like she was licking your dick and enunciating Latin all at the same time. I twitched at the thought of them with the blinds down in the office next door. Did she sit on him? Or did he bend her over the desk and fuck the opinionated out of her?

'Brad,' I grunted, hoping that would limit more conversation.

'How's the new novel coming?'

Jiggle, jiggle. Come on you fucker. 'Fine. How's the gay poetry?'

Irony. Not particularly graspable by Americans. 'Super. Just got a commission from a greetings card company. They tell me it's kinda like Purple Ronnie for over eighteens.'

He said eighteens like *aydeens* and: *Purrrrple Raaaaahnee.* Fucking up our phonemes, pissing on our plosives. I itched with irritation.

'Dunno who this Purple Ronnie character is, do you, man? Big bucks, though.'

'Ah well, that's the main thing, isn't it? The money,' I said. The doorknob turned. Thank Christ.

'Sure is. Catch you at lunch?'

Grunting something about 'bloody tutorials', I closed the door and locked it. You say Asshole, I say Arsehole.

I dropped my briefcase onto the desk and flipped on the lights. It smelled musty from not being used over the weekend, and eyeball-drying hot from the one-temperature-suits-all theory that was cooking the whole university. The bin I'd brought in myself, because the fuckers couldn't bring themselves to provide us with any (because then they'd have to empty it), was still half stuffed. Last Friday's banana skin was decaying sweetly over the lip. I'd shove it down the loo after, or in Brad's pigeon hole.

Rain smattered against the window; I actually found the sound quite comfortable. I cracked it open, looking out onto a school-uniform grey sky, breathing in. Some rain flickered on my cheek, lip, eyebrow. My elemental lover. I smelled bacon and fires. I thumbed on the PC and shook the mini kettle for water, decided there was just about enough, and flicked it on. I ratcheted out the wheelie chair and slumped in it a little harder than I should. My first tutorial wasn't for half an hour and I should be glancing over the student's research questions in preparation for her upgrade panel. But fuck it. I'd wing it.

Brad's comment about the novel pissed me off. Because, obviously, it *wasn't* going well. I decided to temper my frustration, and conscience, by fiddling about with it before the tutorial.

The computer wheezed into life, screen a little dull at first as though sleep-pinched and blinking awake. I imagined some old codger at the back cranking it up, desperate for a first of the morning fag. I fished about in my briefcase for my coffee mug, pulled it out. Karen had substituted it for an Eeyore mug. Silly cow. I grinned and had an image of her in the shower, water hitting the tiles, then patting her hair, padding to the mirror and pulling apart the fan lines at her eyes with thumb and forefinger. She thinks I never catch her. I went to Recent Documents and clicked on *The Lemonade Girl*. My novel splayed out before me, all 521 words of it. And my deadline was next month. And we'd already used the advance to pay for that conservatory in the summer.

Fuck fucking fuck.

I read the words I'd written last May. Right off the back of my first royalty cheque. *The Guardian* called my first book 'inspired'. 'Lamb brings poetry to prose,' says *The Telegraph*. 'Elegant, bare and disturbingly truthful, betraying the marrow in the bones of our prejudices. This is one new writer to watch.' I couldn't remember who that last quote belonged to, or what it particularly meant, but there's nothing like knowing you're being watched to induce a fuck up. My first novel had been about a young, deaf academic discovering the dizzy heights of love, literature and sex. It was utterly pointless, but the publishers whipped up a media buzz and it sold like Cream Eggs in January. Did I, already, have sod-all left to write about? I needed some trauma in my cosy life. My eyes whizzed over the page, mentally moving words about.

Daisy-May is stripping the lemon pips off of her knuckles with her thumbnail, like a knife carving seeds outta peppers. Drawing a wrist cross her forehead, she's gritty-all from the dust-wind. It's getting up strong, she can feel it, like how static crackles through drying bed-sheets touching each other on the line. Zinging down her bones, like all else from Cherrybrook. Daisy-May is born of the earth, the sand and the dust. Mothers will be thumbing patterns in pie crust, wringing grease from their palms, gathering in their daughters and peeking through their shutters for their men folk, who are all but rodeo-riding spooked and bucking cattle to safety in preparation. The heat, it's baking into her chicken-white skin, her chest heavy, sweat making a nest at the back of the tangled candyfloss of her hair, a dew of it balls down her temple, splashes her bare shoulder. Refreshing.

A star winks in the strip-light bright of the day, the star becoming metal which becomes a truck in the flickering distance. Daisy-May is aching for the road, the possibilities it suggests, of getting out of this town.

The truck is rearin up close, chucking up spumes of sand like a raging bull. And Daisy-May, well she's fetchin to leave. But then there was Donovan to think about, and Mickey-Joe. Sweet, good, kind Mickey-Joe with his gravy brains, as momma was want to say, God rest her. Daisy-May knew there was more to him than that, his lumbering figure and baby boy face. If not for him, she could mount up on a shiny white truck and ride out of town, leave her home, Donovan and her past behind.

Daisy-May remains on the dirt, the only girl about in the disintegrating town, resolute at her makeshift stall. Scallops of her lemon skirt twitch against the back of her knees, the stirrer clinking at the neck of the juice jug. Only sound for miles, it seemed.

As the truck slows, the girl with the chicken skin battered in freckles which were not dainty but fat like hundreds of miniature overstuffed cake cases and the lemon scallop skirt, the strangest pink-red candyfloss hair, buffeting in the breeze, as is the jug stirrer, rocked by the sniffing, snuffling exploring wind, whispering of lands far away, picks up her smile as the truck stops in an explosion of hog-squealing metal and grit sparks and says 'Well hey there, sir, y'all thirsty? Got some juice ready. 20 cents a cup.'

'Darlin, I got some juice right here. Won't even charge if you're good.'

'And where is it you be headin, sir?'

'The question missy is where you be headin.'

The dust-wind is creeping strong, stronger and Daisy-Mae stands tall, spine straight as a schoolmistress' cane. The wind pulls back her hair, smoothes over her freckles and curls around her body. The jug stirrer disturbs the buzz of the heat and that sound, that slither inside the dust-wind. It throttles the stirrer livid like a very rattler itself.

Daisy-May reaches out her forefinger, short nails, all practical, and stills the stirrer with a quiet but distinct tink. Her scalloped skirt is uniform, unmoving. The smile gains, eyelashes bat, her lips pull apart. 'Oh no sir, you're quite wrong. That ain't at all the question.'

The truck driver goes bull eyes. He starts for her and it's then the sky does crack.

'Dr Lamb? So sorry, but it is half past. I could come back?'

I wink the document to sleep, net about for a name. 'Jenny!'

She smiles, in that earnest Asian way.

Phew. 'Come. Sit. I was just looking over your abstract.'

'What do you think?'

Fuck. I rub my chin, nodding. 'Why don't we use this session for you to talk, tell me how you're feeling about where you are?' She looked mortified. I'd waste time with a drink. 'Coffee?'

I got through the tutorial, making notes on what Jenny was talking about so I can do some real work and compare it to her abstract at lunch. She started to leave in a blur of clumsiness and nodding. I don't think she blinked the whole time. Some papers go cart-wheeling off my desk.

Again, her total mortification.

'It's fine, really.'

Jenny stoops, swooping everything up. I cop a flash of an almond-coloured bra, scalloped edge like seashells. I cringe. Smooth, plump breasts. Shit. Looking down the top of a girl like this was not remotely like perving on the Greek girl Brad was maybe-fucking. I blushed to match her. Her nail scraped mine as she handed me back some paperwork, leaving a chalk line of white on my skin. The blood drained from my face. The letter. My bowels felt like a grit and porridge mix were extruding through them. I slotted the letter through the mouth of my briefcase. Later.

I nearly put myself to sleep looking at the dull eyes of the students in my Gothic lecture, necks going like rocking horses, never mind the fact I'd snazzed it up with clips from *Buffy* and *True Blood*. After that was the Departmental meeting where I sat like a rocking horse, a spate of tutorials with some MA students and thank fucking finally, home.

I stripped on the way to the shower. Cranking up the heat I stepped in, head back *a la* at the dentist, shower water fizzing on my tongue, gurgling a pool in my throat. I spat. The day washed off me, the heat relaxed my muscles. I pissed in the shower, extra bit of heat on my toes. I dodged. Yellow diluted and disappeared. I found my dick and got hard thinking about the seashell edges of lemon fabric brushing the sensitive place at the back of a girl's knees, an almond bra, fucking Karen as soon as she walked in the door, no questions asked (I blotted out the fact she'd be *mit menschen*). But I was assaulted by that ever-ready pang. It coiled out like smoke before the fire, recharged by the appearance of the letter, unread though it remained: Beth-Anne. I wanked fast and hard, orgasm fired through me. I rinsed myself off and relaxed.

But Beth-Ann…Jesus fucking Christ, girl. Why couldn't I save you?

And then a wall of guilt reared out of the ground, dividing me from Beth-Ann. I almost heard the bricks clank, setting in place. I loved my wife.

'Michael! What're you doing in there building a bleedin' arc?'

I jumped, slopped water in the direction of the last of my cum. Get down. She'd be in any second. I cut the water and picked up a towel. The door cracked and Karen came in, clicking the door closed.

'Munchkins?'

'TV-atonic. I'll rescue them in a mo.' She sniffed. 'You been pissing in the shower again?' She shoved the shower mat closer just in time for me not to step on the cold floor, squirted bleach into the plughole. 'And jobbing off?'

'No? Where did you *learn* that?'

'Michael.'

I scowled. 'I was thinking about you.'

A smile twitched.

I collared her in a hug and kiss. 'We've got time?'

'Ugh. Get off, you're soaking. And it's your turn to cook tea. I've got to get ready for my Tango class.'

I rolled my eyes.

'I saw that. Wouldn't kill you to spend more time with them though, Michael. They miss you.'

'Work…'

'Yeah, I know. But, you know?'

'Mm.'

'I'm always back hot and sweaty though. Set your cock to nine o'clock.'

I laughed, delighted, and pinched her bum as she left with a wiggle of the hips, only to collide with the wall. Karen glanced over her shoulder. 'You didn't see that.'

I laughed harder.

I felt the bed dip as Karen sneaked in late, much later than was usual for her. Her body was tacky with sweat, her hair smelled of cigarettes. She'd been drinking sangria and her toes were ice-cold. I was too dull with sleep to ask why she was so late. The suspicion crept into my lecture the next day. Pinged into it, right between Coleridge and Wordsworth. I faltered, and students wore their rolled-eye looks.

Back in the dry-heat of the office, I felt justified in opening the letter. Karen was keeping something from me, so it was OK. The logic was faultless. I flicked on the monitor, boiled the kettle and sat at my desk. I plucked the letter from the briefcase and set it before me like some meal, or some body up for post-mortem. I tapped my fingers. I picked it up, felt the shape of the folded letter inside the thin envelope, and wondered. A buzz of excitement. Beth-Anne, something of *hers* was inside this envelope. And she wanted something from *me*. I imagined the dust wind from my novel, raging across campus, whispering over my arms and settling in amongst the fine hairs.

My eyes sucked in the words. Some black well of cold tunnelled down inside me, creating a mineshaft. I felt myself plummeting. Oh God. Shit. I'd written this same letter to Beth-Anne over a decade ago. What did this mean? Was Beth-Anne still alive? Was she trying to get a message to me? I felt myself expanding at this idea, my body the balloon and helium hissing in. And then I wondered, What if it wasn't Beth-Anne who'd sent the letter?

A scream ripped up from the quadrangle. Female. I burned with shock and went to the window, a tail of wind tickling my forehead; I was sweating. The student outside giggled, just flirting. Thing is, my gut wasn't any less unsettled. Whoever had sent that letter, they'd also sent me a message. But what did they want and how much did they know?

Impilo

- Jenni Fagan -

I fall backwards into the screech. The lawnmower blades whirr once, twice then gouge into flesh. Muscles sever, bone cracks and splinters; the sky turns white. The motor snarls, its jagged steel teeth rip into sinews, tear at globules of fat and gnaw tissue ragged. Blood arcs slowly up into the vast bleached-out airless nothing. Daffodils nod their heads quietly. The lawnmower sputters to a halt.

Silence.

I am falling.

In the kitchen I see Ama put her mug on the draining board. She looks up and covers her mouth. Between us on the lawn the mowers blades still grind round all spattered in blood and raw lumps of meat. My leg spurts out blood, the severed shin and foot no longer attached. Ama is running down the small back hallway, her bare feet thud off the creaky old floorboards. My severed leg struggles upright; it half turns round to where I lay gasping at it, then it lurches frantically away toward the rosebush. The ankle is purple. Flesh curls away at the calf. One clean shard of bone stabs out the top. The back door whacks open. Ama unwinds her headscarf frantically as she runs and skids down onto her knees.

The toes of the leg wriggle at me.

'It's going to do a tap-dance,' I moan.

'No the fuckin' day it's no.'

Ama rapidly winds her scarf around the stump below my knee, tight, so tight I can feel it through the pain screeching up through my body. The leg hops further away from us. It wavers on the edge of the decking before catching its balance and planking itself firmly down. It bleeds all over the brand new deck that Ama laid for me coming home.

My heart hollers.

The leg tap-dances across to an old cracked mirror behind the peonies and admires its reflection. It turns this way and that to see every bloodied angle. Ama creeps up slowly behind it. She lunges but it bounds out of her reach and pogos furiously through the wild garlic patch, by the bin, then it shuffles right underneath the rose bush.

Just the toes stick out.

Ama pretends to have lost interest and it doesn't move. She whistles, looks at her nails, winks at me, then she turns quick on her heel and launches herself at it, grabbing the thing with both hands. It wriggles as she stands up and holds it out before her as marches inside. Ama brandishes the phone at the kitchen window but I shake my head furiously at her. She won't do it. She won't hand me over. We both know I can't take any more time, I am not going back to jail. We don't need a doctor here. Ama comes back with a duvet. Then there is a pulling, thuds, my sweat slick and cold and the building roar of white noise. I see my dead dog with a leg in its mouth. It runs off through the gate, runs toward the cliffs, the sea.

Everything recedes.

Time leaves; it will have no part in this.

I am laid out in the kitchen, on the chequered linoleum. Ama grabs a rubber hose, snaps it round my arm and yanks hard. She lays out her beach towel, a bottle of gin, her needle kit, some brown, water, morphine she said she didn't have and a saw. She bubbles up some brown in a teaspoon like she never stopped. I thought she'd stopped. Why do you still have the brown, Ama?

'It's OK,' she whispers as she flicks the needle repeatedly, finds a vein and pushes the stopper all the way in. Warm floods through me. She lifts my thigh and leans it straight up against the fridge freezer to slow the bleeding. The wall is smeared with blood. My other leg is folded up against me until I am a half-lotus. She is beautiful, so we float. Ama strokes my hair. A black starless sky whorls through the kitchen door keyhole and drags its weight across me. Ama shrinks. Through a tiny pinprick of light I see her reach for the saw.

I am on the train, it is yesterday and the world is far too wide. Ama Ama Ama the train chugs. As the train crosses the border the windows rattle, way hey!

'Escape?' the tea lady asks me, coffee pot poised.

I look out the window at cliff tops where seven dead girls sway, just like they hung in their cells. Each of them grins widely and waves me on my way.

'Thank you, yes.'

The tea lady pours then shuffles on her way.

In a morgue the seven-suicides-cell girls rub at the red marks around their necks. They snap vertebrae back into place, look at each other and nod.

'She wouldn't have survived much longer,' they say.

'I couldn't do another two years,' the youngest adds.

'You couldn't do another ten minutes,' her sister sniggers.

'Mercy mercy,' they murmur as the morgue man comes to drain their fluids away.

The train smells of beans. It smells of floor. It smells of smelly old man. It does not smell of metal, keys, doors, linoleum, bleach or despair. I will not go back. I won't make it if I do.

I get out at a train station I have not seen for ten years. The marble floor echoes: it seems to ripple like water. A raggedy pigeon hops by; it has one red eye and a slicked-up grease of feathers like a mohawk. The red eye is oozing pus. It looks like one claw is gnarled up, almost growing back into its leg like some weird tumour.

I run up the back steps of the station, air burning at my lungs, out the exit and past some homeless guy, round the corner and she is there and she kisses me again and again. Her hair smells like coconut. I can't stop smiling, this is everything I want. The nine-hour drive to the cottage is me taking in her silhouette, her hand on the gear stick driving like it's so easy. Her laugh light and nervous, our words of mush rolling over each other saying nothing saying I love you—I am here, you are here, this is us again.

The cottage is sixty miles away from anywhere.

The forests are holy. The fields an' gates an' earth an' skies an' brooks an' stiles an' rabbits are holy. Tomorrow I will mow this holy lawn. I will love Ama every single day.

Bits of bone and cartilage drop into the bucket, towels soaked bloody, tissue. Clean gauze soaks in, yellow fluid seeps out. Another needle, more haze. I don't know how many days have passed when I wake. There is a knock knock knock from the porch. Knock, knock, knock, walking sticks getting rattled over, welly boots flung around. That limb was never so active on me. It's like having a puppy.

'What do ye want to do with it?' Ama asks.

'Build a fucking bonfire.'

She takes it up to the bathroom and bathes it in the sink. She reckons I have to say goodbye to it, that I have to take a wee look.

'Or it'll itch and ache,' she calls down the stair. I look up at her and she smiles. 'I saw it in a documentary, there were these people, amputees like, sayin' goodbye tae their limbs on a cushion in a chapel. It helped them accept what had happened. Quite clever eh?'

She is sat on the chair at the top of the stairs patting the leg dry. She knows I'm watching, she sat there with her dressing gown open trying to catch my eye a million times before this all happened, before I went away.

'Chanel black,' she offers as she concentrates, paints each nail carefully. Suddenly I miss my fucking cell. Ama says burning it should be a celebration.

'What is there tae celebrate, Ama?'

'Celebrate ye ever had it in the first place!' she says slowly.

She is clearly insane.

I can smell rotting on what's left of the meat around my kneecap but she's sewn it up neat I'll give her that. Ama says the smell is all in my brain. Toes dried, she wraps a silk scarf round the top of the limb. She cradles it carefully and pads down the stairs barefoot, bare-skinned, kimono flowing. She sits the leg down on a velvet cushion on the table. She has put some glittery shit on it. I wonder if that scarf is long enough to strangle her with. She would look beautiful strangled.

'Look,' she says as she lights candles. I sigh. I look. Despite the glitter an' the Chanel nails an' the velvet cushion an' the candles an' her sitting with her tits out like soon as I need some—she's there: despite all the ceremony that leg looks queasy to me: it looks like it's in drag. Ama photographs the leg with her digital Nikon. I remember when she took Polaroids.

'It's not art,' I state.

'It's all art,' she replies, 'every breath you inhale into yer cells all multiplyin' an' dying an' recreating, it's all art.'

'Like shit in a tin it's art.'

She snorts and begins to laugh so hard she glows. I want to kiss her but first I'd have to punch her and I can't get up yet by myself. Ama's knocked me out some good ones. She trapped my head in the front door once, just trapped it in there, my eyes bulging, shouting, screaming but that was then—then is not now. Now I couldn't touch her wrong no matter how much I might feel like it.

I wake as Ama is lacing a daisy chain anklet round the leg.

'Your barometer of normal is fucked!'

'I never did do normal,' she says.

She's not lying. She never did do normal. She did other stuff, like the piercings through her lip an' her chin an' her clit an' that. She did them by herself as well—sealed the wounds with almost boiling salty water. She's got amazing delicate ornate wee flower tattoos trailing down her belly, round her waist, ornate on her tiny feet. She's lived on a barge, in a shack, a cave and a commune. She's lived in the forest on a platform on stilts where bison ran below each night. A tepee for three years, until she was twenty-three and got left the cottage and it was here that she brought me.

'This place is for us,' she said.

She lavished it with love and made everything grow wild and tall and beautiful, even me. I shouldn't have tried to cut the grass. I shouldn't have had a gin for breakfast. I shouldn't have let Ama meet my Mother in 83. My Mother looked at her like she was some kind of disease made up by some kind of being no-one's even heard of. Ama took it like a real big compliment. Ama isn't keen on normal as an idea. She says that normal is just something they bludgeon you guilty with. She says we're raised to think that normal is a real thing so we police our thoughts and our actions for any aberrations that could outcast us. Ama says that's just how the system wants it, so people keep giving them their money and shut the fuck up. She made stew last night. Greens out the garden. Rabbit out the trap. She told me about her Uncle Willie's scars over pudding. He was stabbed in Glasgow and has scars all over his back, his stomach, his leg and part of his right ear was hacked off.

'An' then there's the masterpiece, a three inch scar right round his wrist.' Ama shakes her head, smiling. 'He wears that scar like a Rolex, like a Rolex he isnae ever takin' off, no until his dyin' day.'

I was twenty-nine when I met Ama an' I'd felt numb my whole life. I never thought anyone could change that. But she did, she's like that, there's always a lot Ama can do. You need a room painted nice, she paints nice. You need someone to help you with something that makes most people sick, call her: nothing can make that girl vomit. You want to talk about them Greek weirdos with the big thoughts, she'll pontificate philosophy till the cows come home. You want to tell someone 'bout something bad and dirty and not feel dumb? Ama'll make you a cup of tea.

She only has one friend.

'One's all I need,' she says.

'What about when Mick dies?' I ask her.

'I just won't see him for awhile,' she says. She reckons if she needs people again she'll go out and find some.

'Plenty of 'em out there,' she states. Ama says the trees are her friends. The ocean, the stars, the sand, the sky, the soup she cooks and the bread she bakes an' the films she cries to with a big smile on her face. My love is enough she reckons.

'You're broke as fuck,' I tell her.

'Nah,' she says, 'I just got lucky that way.'

We wait until nightfall. She gets the wheelbarrow. Puts a duvet in it. Two pillows. Lifts me under the arms. I've had my extra morphine. I feel pretty good all in all. Ama wheels me out the back. The night smells clean and sharp. The stars are so beautiful, so bright and cold looking it makes me feel breathless. I can smell grass and wild garlic and flowers, the scents are crisp like the cold air is preserving them. Ama holds my hand, sits down on an old deckchair. I pull the duvet tight. She hands me a box of matches, I strike a big one and launch it at the bonfire.

Whoosh.

It purrs an' pops right away, the flames crackle and little sparks fly up. The leg begins to sizzle perched there on the top like a fucked bit of meat an' the foot, that foot does not even look like it should be there with its painted nails all shining blackly in the flames. I give it a hard bloody whack with a stick. Ama strokes my hand real gentle and I want to kiss her again. I only need what I need. What I need is all I need. I don't need that limb. I don't. What's weird is that piece of dead flesh burning like a fucking barbecue—it doesn't seem like anything to do with me. My leg feels like it's still here, like at the end of my knee, like I can feel it but it's not there. It's not but somehow it doesn't matter. The fire spits a huge flaming bit of fat out and we both recoil startled.

'Fucking hell,' Ama says slowly, 'that's the last time you help out in the garden.'

I begin to giggle first. It begins with a shaking, in my arms, it comes up through my stomach and I can feel Ama shaking too, wheezing as the laughter comes out. My eyes water and Ama's mouth opens as she laughs and we hold hands totally helpless. The moon stares down at us in a big old silent O. My hand feels good in Ama's. It feels right. Down at the bottom of the garden the old willow tree swishes to and fro, to and fro.

It sounds like waves.

Dick's Life

- Maggie Ling -

My wife slips quietly from our bed, silencing the programmed alarm clock before time, so as not to disturb her sleeping husband. But her husband is awake; I have woken before her, and feign sleep as she moves about the darkened room.

She takes underwear from the chair—removed from the drawer with the jingling brass handles the night before—and pulls on the obligatory panty-girdle: the kind she took to wearing after our daughter was born almost thirty-six years ago, believing the firm support offered by the two-way stretch tummy panel was needed to restore her post-partum body to its pre-partum shape. The girdle, though not needed then, has since become necessary. My wife—seeing no need to change this habit of a lifetime—has several of these corrective garments, washed from virginal snowy whiteness to slush-grey.

She bought some in black once: the two-way stretch satin tummy panel had lines of scarlet stitching running down; a small red bow, attached to its v-shaped centre, rested just below her navel. 'I rather like those,' I said, the first time she put them on. 'More attractive and more practical than white, surely!' 'But I'd have to change all my bras,' she said. And this daredevil piece of decadence, this moment of middle-aged madness, was resigned to a dark corner of the jangly-handled drawer, never to be seen again.

She sits, oh so gently, on the end of our bed. I can see the fuzzy outline of her back: the curved shoulders a little too rounded now, as if she has spent a lifetime wrapping her arms about herself. 'It's the menopause, I expect,' she says. 'There's HRT,' I say. 'Not safe,' she says. And does nothing. 'It's all right for men,' she goes on. 'They don't have to worry about such things'. But does *she* worry about such things?

She fumbles with the hooks of her regulation no frills no fripperies white bra. How would she respond if I put my hand…just there? There in the small of that not-so-small back. If I drew her back into the cooling marital bed, pulled off the warming white dawn-chorus vest that hides her head from me now, tore her ghastly green sweatshirt from her hands, threw those old lavender tracksuit bottoms—that should've been thrown away years ago—across the room and forced her to lay beside me, just for the love of lying there.

She tucks sweatshirt into tracksuit bottoms, bends down for her trainers, and I watch my shadow-play wife tiptoe from the room and, oh so gently, in case she disturbs me, close the bedroom door. Heaven forbid that she should disturb me. At times like this I find it hard to believe she ever did.

I roll over, pull her pillow on top of mine, and watch the dawn light seep in behind the heavy, lined curtains. The pillow still holds her warmth. A dying part of me wants to leap up, scramble into my clothes and follow Gwyneth to the source of her new-found serenity. 'Come with me!' she has said. 'It's something we could share…something positive!' She already knows what I am thinking, already knows what I would never say. 'Come?' she repeats. But I resist, have resisted. And she no longer urges me to share her joy, going alone to meet her fellow twitchers. No longer declaring: 'The spring dawn chorus! To be amongst it. It's *such* a privilege! It's life affirming!'

The last time she urged, 'Come! I promise you'll never regret it.' I almost said, Gwyneth. What if I already do? What if I regret the promise I made to you? What then? Will listening to your feathered friends tweeting across those blue remembered hills make me feel any better? But it's not the sort of thing a man says, is it. Not after almost four decades. Not chivalrous. Not done.

I stretch out my body across no-man's-land. The sheet feels cold. The bed has lost its comforting warmth. I am wide-awake, yet have no wish to move, no wish to stay. I am indifferent. Powerless. Have I always been thus? Was I thus thirty-seven years ago? Neutrality my natural state. Waiting to be conquered—if not by Gwyneth, then by some overwhelming woman; one who might have spewed me out, tired of my passivity. As my wife must frequently tire of me: her lukewarm Laodician.

I look over to the clock. More than three hours have gone by, but still I lie in neutered stupor, my body weighted to the bed.

'Don't worry,' Gwyneth has said. 'It *will* pass. It always does.' She's right. It does. But is she making light of it? Not wanting to expose the *it* that is passing to closer scrutiny. And so she chivvies, she cossets, she chirrups. Twitching, breathing new life into the month of May, for Gwyneth, at least.

I see her coming toward me through the half-light; a slim, flowing form: long hair, long skirt, apache scarf tied around her forehead, trailing down over one shoulder. Something dangling around her neck: beads of some sort. She toys with them, slips them into a knot before slipping them over her shoulder, so that they hang down her straight straight back, so *she* might more easily toy with me. I can just make out a pretty, if unremarkable, face.

My deflowering took place, at the advanced age of twenty-two, in the autumn of 1968, that year of protest and revolt; though I made no timely protest of my own as, in a hazy-daze, my first experience of sexual abandonment sent my virginal petals fluttering to the floor of Bren's bedroom.

Supposedly, one's first sexual experience is, never forgotten. But, after its overwhelming vehemence had died down, I wonder if mine might have faded into the misty memories of my marijuana-fuelled social life, had things turned out differently.

It was another of Bren and Callum's frequent parties. Frequent, largely because, in Bren and Callum's eyes, a party required minimal effort on their part. Food was most certainly not a prerequisite for two guys whose idea of a square meal was four pints of Guinness and a box of Ritz crackers. Bren and Callum's large, eclectic record collection was (at the start of the party, at least), lined up in apple-pie order—the only order in their run-down, messy flat; the front door was wide open to gatecrashers—if sober on arrival; a dozen cans of lager and a wine box were in the fridge, a stash of weed and skins in the sitting room and—if they were *really* pushing the boat out—one or two packets of crisps and a few peanuts had been thrown into half a dozen chipped bowls and dotted about the place.

Whilst still in my virginal state, I vaguely recall a pleasant time spent in the kitchen; an incongruous chunk of Parmesan cheese had been found, lurking behind a wine box in the fridge, and after the green crust had been pared from it, cheese, knife, and current joint were passed around the group, each one of us coming up with increasingly bizarre theories as to why such an exotic comestible could have found its way to Bren and Callum's refrigerator. I cannot recall a single face from that group, just hands passing one to the other—Gwyneth's may well have been amongst them. Perhaps she had already set her cap at me? (Though that contraceptive turn-off came later!)

Back then, in Bren and Callum's food-free kitchen, I was a carefree, sexless zone, at one with my solitary self, with no desire to spread my seed hither and thither.

As a boy I had used the conventional method of relief to good effect and, aided by a selection of top-shelf stimulation had continued in this way to my complete satisfaction. But I had yet to be blessed by the white-breasted whirlpool of sexual energy that was Gwyneth Bronwen Jones, to be consumed by her Charybdian charms, to be drowning inside her.

And so it happened that, while my college chums were high and happy, laying any swinging, pill-taking chick they could lay their carefree hands on, I was venturing where no twenty-three-year-old should ever go, moving not *out* of, but *into* suburbia! My feet reluctantly placed on this ladder of life courtesy of Gwyneth's affluent parents. My new wife and I ensconced in a pleasant, tree-lined avenue, which—and I cannot recall if this is fact or fiction—in my memory had a burial ground at its end; it was, appropriately, a cul-de-sac!

I see my pregnant wife shuffling about our pride and joy: a snazzy fitted kitchen. I see her hands massaging the enlarging bump. 'Our bump!' she would say. Why *our* bump? The bump was patently in her body. The bump was cooed over in Gwyneth's Welsh wood-pigeon coo. The bump was caressed more often by her hands than by my own. *She* had been the force of its creation.

Gwyneth had decided our snazzy kitchen drawers must be lined with wipe-clean Contact. I see her cutting along the red-lined grid, see her peeling back the backing paper, smoothing the green and white check, scattered with yellow lemon slices, on to the bottom of the cutlery drawer. Somehow this banal memory cannot be wiped away. I see myself, watching from one of the two uncomfortable stools, thinking: This cannot be happening. This cannot be *my* life! This cannot be the woman who, a mere eight months ago, overwhelmed me at Bren and Callum's—

to all intents and purposes, raped me! This…*Stepford* wife must be an impostor. I have to escape! I have plans! Dreams! If only that guy in the kitchen hadn't run out of cigarette papers…

I'd gone to Bren's bedroom to get another packet of Rizlas from my coat pocket. Not bothering to turn on the light, I am searching through the mound of coats when I hear the door close, oh so gently, behind me. I turn to see a murky form coming toward me, and feel pleasantly disturbed. And, suddenly, I'm on top of the mound, and the murky form's on top of me. On top of me like she couldn't wait, like she'd been working up to this moment for quite a while. I can hardly breathe, half suffocated by sheepskin, the brass buttons of someone's Sergeant Pepper jacket grinding into my back with every groan this unknown whirlwind emits.

Was it really *my* Gwyneth who uttered those three little words all men long to hear? 'You're *still* hard!' Before slipping from me, dropping her long fringed-skirt to her ankles, and floating silently from the room. Leaving me in post-coital daze, my duck broken, my dick smarting with a more satisfying kind of satisfaction.

Perhaps, I've sometimes thought, if she had stayed, had lain beside me, doe-eyed and adoring, giving me one of those where-do-we-go-from-here looks, my whole life might've been different. She might have remained forever the unknown woman of my first lay. But this woman appeared not to give a damn. Appeared to be of the she saw, she came, she conquered and she left variety; a wicked, quick-shag-queen of the night kind of woman. Every twenty-something's wet dream! Though I suspect, even whilst shagging me in the sheepskin, there might've been a hint of the puppy-dog and slippers stratagem nestling in Gwyneth's subconscious, because, as it turned out, this particular conquest wasn't just for Christmas. It was for life!

I stagger to my feet, begin buttoning up my flies, to find her pants hooked around a button, attached by their label: Saint Michael; turquoise blue cotton knit, a hint of minimal lace around the legs; nothing to get excited about; nothing to get off on. I should've seen those knickers as a bad sign. On the surface the sexy siren. Beneath bog standard knickers. Knickers not used to regular exposures at orgies, unaccustomed to being hooked around a slain fella's fly button.

I believe it's said a woman doesn't reach her sexual peak until her mid-thirties, while my poor sex, sad unfortunates that we are, begin slithering down the flaccid slopes to impotence from the innocent age of eighteen.

Gwyneth's Ben Nevis moment came that October evening; she was nineteen.

Gwyneth is cotton knit through and through. I have never been able to wean her off its utilitarian comfort. Though I have tried.

One birthday, about fifteen years ago, I gave her an expensive pair of French knickers: red silk—a hint that we might spice up our flagging sex life. She wore them once. 'But,' I asked, 'didn't they feel nice against your skin?' 'They cut into my crotch,' she replied. 'How could that feel nice?' And soon they joined the black panty girdle, somewhere in the nether regions of Gwyneth's underwear drawer.

Gwyneth has never been quite the same down there, in that furry foreign country, since Claire's birth. A hatchet job made of the episiotomy. Done in haste because 'baby' was in foetal distress. Or so Gwyneth told me. I was dashing through the city to Waterloo station as my wife's waters broke. 'Baby' arrived too early. Husband arrived too late. Too late to see my only child breeching its way into the world. Too late to witness Gwyneth's perineum being mutilated by a pair of pinking shears! 'Obviously, sex is best avoided,' the midwife informed us. 'For a little while, at any rate. But, after a few weeks, everything should be fine down there.' Well she got that one wrong, too, didn't she. Sex was off the agenda for months. Or was it years? It certainly felt like it. Though, episiotomy or not, I doubt that either of us was up for it anyway.

As the bump had grown, as our proto-baby began to make her disruptive presence felt, so Gwyneth grew overprotective—a mother's intuition, you might say. She said sex felt uncomfortable. Didn't feel 'quite right'. She said it might 'harm the baby'. 'That's bollocks!' I said. 'The baby'll be fine!' 'What do *you* know?' she said.

Nothing at all, it seems.

I used to wonder what might have happened if Gwyneth *hadn't* become pregnant? We had a pretty good time at the beginning. Even *after* we were married: before the bump became too big. Our honeymoon was quite a bed-in. Could have knocked John and Yoko's into a cocked hat. Not Amsterdam, but Nice: a nice family-run hotel, familiar to, and generously paid for by, Gwyneth's affluent parents (keen as they were to welcome me to the bosom of their family). It was hot stuff down there. My whirlpool wife, as warm and inviting as a Jacuzzi, bubbling over my accepting body—with a *little* less furiosity.

Naively, the fact that the maelstrom's knickers couldn't have twisted themselves around my fly button never occurred to me. I stuffed them into my pocket, giving my skinny profile added pizzazz, and joined the partying throng.

About half an hour later, through the smoky haze of the hall, I see her standing by the bathroom door. 'Hi there,' she says, shuffling from one foot to the other. 'Wish whoever's in there would get a move on. I am *desperate*!' 'I've got something you might need,' I say, pulling her pants from my pocket. 'You certainly have,' she says, and pulls me in with her. I watch her pee. Watch her wipe her unmutilated fanny with the turquoise knickers, Bren and Callum's hospitality not quite stretching to the additional bog-roll required by female party-goers. 'Don't need these, do I?' she says, looking up at me, doe-eyed. I watch her flush them down the loo. Feel her mouth envelope mine…And we do it again, there in the bathroom. I turn on the tap to muffle her expressive moans: the hot one, by mistake, and pretty soon we can't see each other for steam. And Callum's banging on the door screaming: ' If whoever's in there is so *fucking* desperate for a soddin bath, they can go down the soddin road to The Porchester Halls! Not drain our soddin gas meter dry!'

I reach out to illuminate the clock: seven forty-five; Gwyneth will soon be home. With effort I drag my torpid body to the window and pull back the curtains. Blinding spring sunshine fills the room. My squinting eyes look down at the garden. Black-stemmed bamboo sways in a gentle breeze, tulips, the colour of ripe plums, poke their heads through a sea of custard yellow euphorbias. And I marvel at my wife's artistry, at her ability to weave this changing tapestry of texture and colour from plug and pot, seed and sapling, envy her ability to find this conduit for her prodigious love.

We moved here twenty-six years ago. For Claire's sake. A place had come up at a good school nearby—we still had hopes for our daughter, then. 'You're very fortunate,' we were told. 'Such places are like gold dust!'

How lucky we were!

Gwyneth soon put the little energy she had left into bringing the neglected garden back to life. And as Gwyneth nurtured the garden, the garden nurtured Gwyneth. I watched my wife, if not blossom, then at least regain some of her vigour, a faint bloom returning to her cheeks. 'It's meditative,' she informed me. 'I forget everything when I'm out there. If it works for me…?' But, I was still a young man! I was *only* thirty-five! I felt *my* biological clock had been tampered with. Felt my life hurtling toward middle age, old age, toward death. 'How *can* we forget?' I yelled. 'How in *heaven's name* can we!' She brushed a tear from her cheek, put on her gardening gloves and walked out to the terrace. It was May, of course. A month that Gwyneth has learned to love. But May can still bring the black dog howling at my door.

I go into the bathroom, turn on the shower, and see her through the steam; remember those blue eyes, their dilated pupils a nose-tip from mine, see her slip the bandana from her head, moistened blonde waves rippling over her face.

'Hi there, hard man,' she says, 'I'm Gwyneth!' And Callum's still banging on the bathroom door as this woman is adjusting my equipment and, oh so skilfully, buttoning up my flies, in a way that suggests she has done this many times before.

'You couldn't be more right,' I say. 'I'm Richard: Richard Hardmann.'

'Well, hello Dick!' she says, slithering down on her haunches to kiss my crotch, looking up. 'Can I call you Dick?' She stretched her arms around my neck, swinging her legs around my waist, kissing me long and hard.

'I'd rather you didn't,' I say when I get my breath back.

And we cling together in the clearing steam, our bodies hot and damp, her naked fanny pressed against my half-buttoned crotch, my hands supporting her smooth-skinned buttocks, in silent, reckless oneness, until she says: 'So! How do we get out of here? Is there a window we could escape through?'

'Nope!' I say. 'We'll have to open that door and face the music! There *is* no escape.'

How right I was.

'She's a gift from God, all the same. *All* children are,' my mother informs me, when I telephone with the news that her beautiful new grandchild is destined to remain a child for the rest of my mother's grandparental life, adding: 'But, of course, you'll try again soon, won't you?'

Not *quite* such a gift, then.

It was around the time of my puberty, at the start of my long passage to adulthood, that my own stealthy fumblings under the candlewick caused me to consider my fate as an only child; an only child whose mother confessed to being a 'strict' Catholic.

An early memory of my mother is of her at the lunch table: her long neck stretched up, her eyes gazing beyond the cracked ceiling rose and the dusty glass chandelier, to Our Father's spotless home on high. Then, chin lowered, her closed eyes cast down to hands clasped in benediction, an incantation was uttered over the food before us. This only serving to make me suspicious as to the contents of my lunch. My mother, I concluded, rightly unsure of her culinary powers, had seen fit to plead for assistance from the Lord should her family be struck down after consuming the pea and ham soup she had prepared, and, as a consequence, the contents of my bowl remained untouched.

Though, that evening, when both parents appeared in robust health at the supper table, I deemed it safe to consume the tiniest piece of tinned salmon. This regime of limited sustenance continuing for several days, until I became satisfied I would not be poisoned by my mother's kitchen sorcery (nor by God's). And thus grew to skinny, suspicious pubescence (believing my mother to be poisoned, nonetheless).

She would attend daily mass; she would light her candle; she would go to confession. And I would wonder what it was she had to confess—save for the two almighty sins of overcooked cabbage and lumpy custard—while coming to realize that my mother was right in one respect. For she was *laden* with guilt: the guilt of embracing the Lord and of *not* embracing life. Life was borne out with a sufferance by my mother. Life was what she had been forced to go through in order to return to her Father again, since we were all *gifts* from him in the first place. A gift of the worst kind: a gift with conditions attached. No gift at all, in fact.

I would also wonder—good Catholic that she was—why my mother had not managed to deliver a few more gifts for me, her only son: one or two ribbon-tied sisters; two or three tag-playing brothers. Denial, I concluded, had played a large part in my mother's life. A self-denial, should she still desire my father, or a privation of sexual pleasure denied my father, should *he* still desire her. Or else an unspoken *dis*avowal of her supposed 'beliefs'.

A further option later occurred to me (one deemed too depressing to consider in those drab years of my childhood): the possibility that my parents no longer loved each other enough for the whole risky business of sex ever to take place.

For, amongst her 'God-given gifts', the gift of love was not heavily bestowed upon my mother. Claire, our precious little 'gift', was only a gift in my mother's eyes so long as Claire remained little. My mother could not adjust to the awkward lumpen teenager, to the overweight dribbling adult her grandchild became. But who am I to cast stones? I wouldn't visit our daughter for weeks on end—months, at one point. To the extent that Gwyneth gave up urging me to do so. While she would drive there almost every day: to wipe the drool from Claire's mouth, to spoon the baby-mush lunch into the mouth that would have to be wiped all over again. On one or two occasions Gwyneth insisting our fifteen year old child had uttered the word 'Mumma'. Straws in the wind. Imagined sparks to lighten the gloom.

I should've gone with Gwyneth more often. The guilt remains. But then, I'd never declared, never faintly considered, the ghastly trick of fate that was our daughter 'a gift' as my mother had done.

I think my parents were attracted to the idea of living out their last years in Spain largely because it was a long way from their grandchild. A gift-wrapped present twice a year was all the God-given-love they could handle after Claire hit twenty-one. And it didn't look quite so ludicrous, or feel *quite* so embarrassing, to fold pretty paper around that Farmer John animal puzzle, or that Bumper Colouring Book, knowing the postman would deliver it for you.

I dress slowly and go downstairs.

In the kitchen Gwyneth has put coffee in the pot, ready on the stove, and croissants in their tin, waiting to be heated: our Sunday-breakfast treat. The Burgundy brochures are on the table. 'Richard,' she'd said. 'We *must* decide this weekend!'

'Love is a hard taskmaster,' Gwyneth once said, when I suggested she ease up on her visits to Claire. Was I jealous of her ability to give love? Or resentful, because of my own *in*ability.

I used to fantasize a different life. One completely under my control.

I meet a woman, in full curvaceous bloom, whom *I* overwhelm, who succumbs instantly to my charms, whom I leave, panting for more. To do the same the next day, with a different woman, and the next, with another, and the next, and the next, with no responsibility, no consequences…with no love.

Ten days in Burgundian wine country. 'It'll be a birthday present for you!'

'But Gwyneth,' I say. 'There's Claire…?'

Since those carefree days before my twenty-second birthday, this annual day of celebration has become a source of sadness to me. For an extra birthday gift arrived—seemingly in good order—just two days after the anniversary of my own birth. Though that second bottle of champagne, purchased for our special delivery (expected to arrive in early

June), was left unchilled.

Gwyneth, unconvinced by the midwife's stamp of perfection, was, she confessed, more prepared for the news than was I. A mother's instinct, she said.

For better or worse, I go with Gwyneth, now, as often as I can, and *always* on Claire's birthday. For some time our daughter came home for the day. But even Gwyneth had to admit Claire had become too big a baby for her. Now we spend the day there—well, midday until seven-thirty, when they usually put Claire to bed. Gwyneth reads her a bedtime story, then we slip away, feeling we've done our duty.

'We'll go see Claire the weekend before,' Gwyneth says. 'She's hardly going to notice the difference, is she. *We* need a break, Richard. We've each other to think of.'

I hear her car on the gravel, light the coffee, turn on the oven, and reach the corner of the terrace as she comes through the side gate. She's smiling as she walks toward me, her body swaying in the same girlish way that, in spite of everything, she has never lost, the face beneath the extra pounds still pretty, in that unremarkable way, and, I think, more interesting now that suffering has etched depth into it. She wraps a green sweatshirted arm around my waist and we walk in silence into the kitchen.

'Did you sleep better last night?' she asks, putting butter and milk on the table. 'I hope I didn't disturb you.'

'No,' I lie. 'And yes, I slept better. I'm surfacing.'

Her hand strokes my shoulder. 'It always passes, doesn't it,' she says, softly, stooping to check on the croissants, while I watch a peacock butterfly, wings spread out on the brick wall outside the kitchen door, its jewel colours glinting in the sunshine.

'We must book this *now!*' She flutters the fan of brochures under my nose. 'You may be able to say no to the birds and the bees, but not, I *know*, to a decent drop of Burgundy.' She flashes me a cheeky smile, and we are back in Bren's bedroom, we are there with Callum banging on the bathroom door, and I smile too—for the first time in weeks!

She puts the tray of crisped croissants on the table, raises a warm hand to my cheek, and says, 'That's it, Dick. Keep that pecker up!' And the touch is not sexy, but soft, the look not lust, but love. And I feel hope returning. It always does!

Gwyneth pours coffee into our Sunday coffee bowls (bought on a trip to Brittany two years ago) and I feel the black dog skulking away. It gives a pathetic growl before slinking to the door. Perhaps it might stay away forever if I learn to growl back, if I don't roll over and allow myself to be conquered by it.

'Did you say you wanted to go to the garden centre today?'

'Yes. But I can pop there myself, in my car.'

'Mine's got a bigger boot!'

She looks so pleased, so grateful. I kick the drooping dog still lurking on the terrace. It yelps. I feel a sense of power.

'It's beautiful out there,' I say, 'I'd like us to share the day.'

I hear it whimper, and watch it limp away into the bright May morning.

Parallax

- Tessa West -

Background

> *The part of the scene that appears behind the principal subject of the picture.*

Justin, my Head of Department, was waving the *Times Educational Supplement* at me as he approached. 'Cassie, look at this! There's a job here that fits you perfectly!'

He made me stand right there in the corridor and read the ad he'd ringed.

LEARNING MANAGER—VISUAL ARTS AND MEDIA
Visualise yourself as a leader

The Bath School of Art and Design has more than 300 full-time students on programmes ranging from level 1 through to BA(Hons) Degree. It has two dedicated Art School campuses.

> *This post is an opportunity to become a Curriculum Learning Manager with a remit to manage the Further Education side of the school based at the Southwood House campus. You will also work closely with, and have opportunities to teach on, the Higher Education courses at the Blair campus.*

Justin was right: at this stage of my career it was perfect. I had plenty of experience in FE and was hungry to extend into HE; I'd been in my present college for five years so it was the right time to make a move; the college at Bath was bigger than the one I was in and it had a good reputation; and having grown up in Bristol I knew the area quite well. I couldn't have asked for anything better.

'Have you seen this bit? *"We are looking for a motivated and ambitious individual who specialises in art or design and who can manage, and lead, the Creative curriculum and staff."* I don't want to see you go but that's you to a T, isn't it? The closing date is in six weeks, so you've got plenty of time.'

I nodded, but I knew already that Neil would not want me to apply and that nothing would make him change his mind in six years, let alone six weeks. He'd say we both had perfectly good jobs, the children were settled in decent schools and that we'd finally got the house as we liked it. He was right, of course, and when I went home and tried to discuss the idea he just closed down and wouldn't budge.

Reciprocity
    Most films are designed to be exposed within a certain range of exposure times. When exposure times fall outside this range a film's characteristics may change. These changes are called reciprocity effect.

After ten days of stalemate I'd reached the point where I wanted to take him by the shoulders and force him to face me, make him engage with me.

Did he want us to stay as we were for ever? Did he want us to live in the same house and remain in the same jobs for ever? Were we never—not even one of us—to step beyond our present lives and extend ourselves a bit? Of course the children needed stability and continuity, but it wasn't as if I was suggesting we should move every three or four years.

'So where would that leave me?' he had asked, and I'd answered that because Bath was a lot bigger than Bury St Edmunds he'd find work easily.

On Saturday, I brought the subject up again when Zak was at football practice and Martha up in her room.

'For God's sake! Stop going on about that bloody job.' Neil turned on the tap and filled the kettle noisily.

I was shocked. I had never shut him up when he wanted to talk about something important, and I never would. And nor had he ever done it to me.

'I'm only asking you to consider it instead of dismissing it out of hand.'

'I have.'

'You haven't. You seem to have a problem with the idea of progress.'

'Progress? How can you be so sure changing jobs and moving house is progress?' Neil wetted his finger and started picking up single grains of spilt sugar from his saucer and transferring them to his tongue.

Angle of View
The area of a scene that a lens covers or sees.

I tried again. 'Of course you'd find a job. There'll be plenty of opportunities for lawyers in Bath.'

'I've told you before, you haven't a clue about careers in my particular field.'

'Why not ask Ian, or Des? They'll know, or they'll know who could advise you. Actually, I'll be seeing Des tomorrow at the badminton club so...'

'*No*. Don't say anything. Can't you see how that could jeopardise my position?'

'Neil, for God's sake. He's our *friend*.'

'He's also my employer.'

I began to peel some onions. Why was he so resistant? Was he really scared of stepping outside his usual territory? Why did he have to be so difficult?

'I'm going to fetch Zak.'

Neil put on his coat, picked up the car keys and went out. I took the sausages out of the fridge, pricked them and arranged them on the oven tray.

'What's the matter, Mum?'

I turned to see Martha standing by the door. She must have just come in.

'Why did you sigh like that?'

'Did I sigh?'

'Yes.'

'I need a big hug.' She ran over and hugged me hard. Her head came to just above my waist, just below my ribs.

She said, 'I can hear your heart.'

I said, 'Good. That's very good news,' which made Martha laugh and prevented me from crying.

As I stroked her hair I looked at the photo on the shelf behind her. It was taken on our honeymoon in Italy. Neil had asked a couple who happened to be passing by to take a photo of us. The man agreed at once, so Neil gave him the camera and hurried back to me. He put his arm round my shoulder and I put my arm round his waist. In the background was a villa and I suddenly recalled how when we had touched its wrought iron gate we had almost been burned by its heat.

'That's better. Right, let's lay the table now.'

Hyperfocal Distance
Distance of the nearest object in a scene that is acceptably sharp when the lens is focused on infinity.

After lunch Neil announced he was going to have a major raking up of leaves and light a bonfire. The children were keen to help and by two o'clock the three of them were out there in their coats and boots.

I didn't mind clearing up the meal on my own, but as I did it I was seething about Neil's negativity. He refused to discuss it properly, wouldn't do more than say no. No, he wasn't going to move. No, he wasn't going to change his opinion. No, he wasn't going to visit Bath and have a look around. I felt exhausted.

Fogging
Darkening or discolouring of a negative or print or lightening or discolouring of a slide.

He had opposed me at other times but this was the worst. He had been set on buying this house even though it meant having a very heavy mortgage which he often complains about. He refused to let me buy the Fiat I wanted and insisted I have the car he found through a friend. And two years ago he disapproved of the way I'd taken up a section of lawn to make room to grow vegetables.

'But we spend loads on organic vegetables,' I protested. 'Why not grow them here in our own back garden?'

'You'll get fed up with it. You'll always have to be out there adding compost or weeding or setting traps for slugs.'

Filter
> *A coloured piece of glass or other transparent material used over the lens to emphasize, eliminate, or change the colour or density of the entire scene or certain areas within a scene.*

I feel as if I just can't win. Not that I want to *win*, exactly, but I can't cope with this blocking, this refusal to shift.

Do I shut *him* off? Am I as unsatisfactory for him to be with as he is for me? Is it *me* rather than him who's got things wrong?

I thought about his photography. He's mad about photography and has been the secretary of the Bury St Edmunds Camera Club for five years. It's occurred to me more than once that perhaps he prefers to see life through a lens. People phone him up all the time for advice and he goes out of his way to help them, even complete beginners. And he's always finding out about new equipment and new techniques, always working out ways round problems.

So is it just me he's at loggerheads with? And if so, is it my fault?

Needing peace and space I walked down the garden. Martha was filling up a wheelbarrow with armfuls of leaves and Zak was poking the bonfire with a stick.

'Dad says we can cook potatoes in the embers later on,' said Martha.

Neil must have seen me coming but he didn't look up from his raking, so I told him I was going out for a walk.

I didn't expect him to reply but he said, 'I've been thinking. If you're so determined to apply for that job then apply for it. But if you get it don't expect me and the kids to come with you.' Then he started to rake again.

I stepped over the ditch and into the field. The earth was covered with a thin layer of green winter wheat. There was a scattering of black rooks.

Parallax

Depth of Field

The amount of distance between the nearest and farthest objects that appear in acceptably sharp focus in a photograph.

It felt as if he had hit me. Surely he didn't mean what he'd said? Surely things weren't that bad?

I followed the edge of the field, my boots heavy with mud, through the gateposts that no longer held a gate and so into another field which I crossed to reach the western end of Tinker's Wood. I came here often; sometimes to think, sometimes to worry and sometimes just to walk. Although it was part of a private estate no one minded me going there and I thought of it as my wood.

He was like a wall. A solid wall with no way through. But he wasn't seriously suggesting that we split up, was he?

The wood's a dark place in summer, but winter lets the light in.

Ambient Light

The available light completely surrounding a subject.

You can always see pheasants and rabbits here, and occasionally squirrels. I've never yet found a fox or a badger, but you often come across deer. I've seen muntjac hardly bigger than adult hares, does bounding through the brushwood and once in the rutting season I tracked a harsh bark to a big stag alone in a clearing. Even though a road runs past the eastern edge of the wood I've rarely seen people here, not even in spring when there's swathes of wild garlic and the twigs are laden with catkins.

Although I was hurting I didn't feel like crying, more like yelling.

I always walk carefully in the wood, and every now and again I stop and listen, but that day I realised I was marching along not noticing anything.

So I made myself stand still until my breathing slowed down. Gradually I felt calmer. Gradually, as I took in the trees and the bushes I was able to let go of our arguments and my frustration and pain. All that was left was a dull feeling.

As I stood there I heard something unusual and sensed movement. It wasn't a snuffling, or a scraping or a scratching. It was too big a sound for a bird or birds. Was it a deer rubbing itself against a tree—which I've

150

never seen—or could it be a person? I walked on, very slowly, very softly.

The noise was ahead of me which was odd, because the path was unprotected and the wildlife is usually amongst the trees to the left and right rather than in the open.

Then, at the same moment as I recognised the rasping sound to be uneven breathing, I saw something move at the very edge of the path, half in a dry ditch.

As I got closer I made out a deer on its side, so I waited for it to jump up and away, but it didn't. Closer still, and I saw there were two deer. Strangely, legs were poking out at unnatural angles.

Selective Focus

Choosing a lens opening that produces a shallow depth of field. Usually this is used to isolate a subject by causing most other elements in the scene to be blurred.

I approached to within ten feet before I realised that the antlers of the two deer were locked together. They must have been fighting and fallen and found they couldn't extricate themselves. One was breathing hoarsely and the other was dead. I touched each hide in turn, one warm, one cold. I looked into the eyes of the live deer and it blinked. After being trapped for hours—probably overnight from the look of it—it was giving up. Exhausted, hungry, thirsty and in pain, it was beyond terror.

These weren't young bucks who had been play-fighting but mature adults determined to establish their status and territory. Some bizarre misfortune had resulted in them being held by and holding the other in an intimate deadlock which I tried to shift but couldn't. They were the same size and I wondered whether they were brothers. Perhaps they had even lain in the womb together.

I would have to phone the estate forester.

As I hurried home I felt increasingly that I wanted Neil to experience what I had experienced. I was relieved to find the children had gone inside so I could speak to him on his own. He was forking round the outside of the dying fire, pulling the edges into the centre.

'They're tangled up?'

'Yes. It's horrible, but it's extraordinary too. And it's important.'

'What do you mean?'

'It's important for us. It means something. I want you to see what's happened.'

He jabbed his fork into the ground and pulled off his gardening gloves.

'OK. I'll get my camera.'

Parallax

With a lens-shutter camera, parallax is the difference between what the viewfinder sees and what the camera records, especially at close distances.

The Soul of Cinema

- Karen Whiteson -

Of course, I'd thought, on first spotting him earlier, during Registration, Irwin Kohn would be here, wouldn't he? For Irwin was nothing if not ubiquitous. Possessed of the small, clever man's terror of being overlooked, he'd a whole array of devices by which to ensure visibility: his ecstatic lapdog gurning and sanctimonious aura of One Who Serves—not to mention the heel to throat blue denim outfit he wore day in day out. (The students had a running joke that he was a blue-denim rag doll who could never get undressed). Irwin was Irwin: he was, if not quite a national treasure, certainly an institutional fixture. He was, after all, God's representative on Earth of the film-making avant-garde: the historic, analogue, avant-garde: those makers of radical celluloid and video, who were back in the spotlight.

Now, I found myself plonked behind Irwin's shiny pate, ringed by its trademark dark frizzy halo. I shouldn't have gone to that Habitat sale, I thought; it had made me late back from lunch. Most of the conference-goers had returned and the speaker was already in full flow when, carrier dangling from one hand, takeaway coffee in another, I'd come in. I had hovered a moment or two in the doorway, nervously scanning the auditorium, then made my way up to the back where I'd stalled again.

Someone sitting at the end of the row had stood up and gestured for me to go through and, scared of dithering, I complied. Apart from the polite stranger, it was empty. I divested myself of my shopping and sat there sipping coffee, tuning into the lecture:

'Today we have to re-interpret where film happens. It's a matter of windows onto filmic experience. We need to think in terms of the relocation of cinema.'

I bent down to rummage through my bag for a notebook and pen. It was only as I sat back up and found myself facing the back of Irwin's head, that I clocked my unfortunate position. He must have seen my entrance and possibly even thought Ah, here comes Lydia, making a deliberate beeline for me.

I gazed woefully before me, noting that Irwin was, as per usual, flanked by cronies; the woman on the left resembling a female version of him: same dark frizz (though minus bald spot) plus same inquisitive beak of a nose. I didn't know her name as she had appeared on the scene after I had left the College; but, on the few occasions I'd run into Irwin since, he invariably had this mystery look-a-like of his in tow.

Now that I had clocked it, it was hard not to stare at the back of Irwin's skull. For respite now and again I shut my eyes. How did this happen? I know I should have remembered this was going to happen, I thought. For I couldn't help but recognise the moment as a troublesome old friend, which I should have seen coming. For the rest of the afternoon I heard only fragments of the talk, which seemed to free float, divorced from their speaker, filtered through the haze of anxiety.

'...the close-up, variously defined as "the soul of cinema" or "the psychological shot" or "a cellular revelation"—the close-up is said to have "the power of prognostication. In the future, instead of horoscopes, the more credulous demographic will consult the close-up."'

As I opened my eyes, my gaze rested on the inevitable object before me, beads of sweat forming on its surface.

'The close-up is not a shift into narrative stasis, but into another temporality reflecting the tempo of subjective experience. The close-up as window onto embodied subject which gives us a lyrical moment, polyphonic and simultaneous.'

Beyond Irwin's head, a silent movie showed Lillian Gish joyfully announcing her pregnancy to her husband. Then he was telling her that he was already married and that their contract was therefore null and void.

'As the expectant wife struggles to grasp that she is in fact a fallen woman, her expression transmutes from joy to horror to joy to horror—her face so split by this impossible moment that it seems to simultaneously exist in two separate time zones.'

Watching that fractured face I found myself wondering if it is true that tomorrow some catastrophic event may occur, then what does that mean today, now, in this moment? Either the catastrophe will occur, in which case my present sense that it may not happen is unsound; or, it does not occur; in which case my sense it might is mistaken and my grasp of the present, skewed.

As the houselights went up again, Irwin produced a handkerchief and mopped his pate, brow and behind-the-collar area while his mystery lady poured Lucozade into a plastic cup and passed it to him with a concerned tilt of her head. It wasn't really that warm in the auditorium. Irwin's heat must be generated by a more internal source. Was it a reaction to the sight of Lillian Gish running the emotional gamut from A to Z? Or, maybe it was because of my inadvertent proximity, which meant he could no longer avoid the fact he was being avoided by me?

It was only that morning, on first spotting him at the registration desk, cup and saucer in hand, working double-time to exude geniality in all directions, that it had dawned on me why Irwin was so averse to my blanking him. His function within the College was essentially that of a gossip machine and I was depriving his mill of its grist. I was simply withholding all anecdotal behaviour. So that, if asked he'd properly be able to do nothing but give a desultory shrug and hope to acquit himself with that. Or, if pressed, he might find himself having to confess to having been ignored by me.

Big deal. All this merely supplied the habeas corpus for the real question: why did it matter if a fair to middling-sized banana like Irwin was ignored by a relative nonentity like me? And, more to the point, so far as I was concerned, who on Earth did it matter to?

About this I was insanely curious. My withholding from Irwin was not merely pique, it was also a way of calling his bluff. If Irwin was pantomiming perplexity, wasn't it because he felt himself robbed of some anecdotal trophy which he sorely needed in order to maintain his status quo, in the eyes of the one who had conferred it upon him in the first place i.e. his Boss, Professor of Graphic Design aka BF?

At the highest estimate and the highest estimate only—Irwin's attentions supplied circumstantial proof of his Boss's interest in me. But Irwin had turned out to be a dishonest broker and so I had decided to reject the messenger (though, not the message). But this theory of Irwin as go-between *manqué* wanted continual testing if I was to persuade myself I was not merely in thrall to some private fantasy.

The conference was coming towards the end. I did not want to still be sat there when Irwin stood up so I gathered up my stuff and, with an apologetic look, sidled past the polite stranger. I found a seat in the very back row which, apart from a slumbering academic, was unoccupied.

My secret notion was that I was the recipient of a message from BF. Now that I'd left the place where he worked, my illustrious friend was using the media to maintain contact. Mainly it was a matter of certain select radio programs and print columnists who acted as BF's spokespeople. It all made perfect sense to me on some level, so long as I did not have to try to explain it to anyone else, for that was when, to mine own ears, I began to sound like someone severely bipolar ranting on about their influencing machine.

Muffled through a veil of stupefaction, I heard a speaker announce a coffee break before re-adjourning for the final set of lectures and re-settled myself in my seat with the intention of continuing my reverie. Drifting off, I realised there was somebody looming over me.

'I don't know if you're aware of how disruptive you were being with all that rustling of papers...?' said the woman standing there.

I didn't know her, but in my soporific state she resembled someone else, who I did know, who happened to be at the conference.

'Because you were making an awful lot of noise with those papers,' she went on.

That cursed Habitat carrier, I thought. 'Awfully sorry,' I said.

'I only mention it in case you were wondering why people kept on. Looking. Round. At. You.' She gave an encompassing gesture hinting at the entire auditorium's worth of disapproval.

'Right. So now, quite rightly, you are chastising me. So I stand chastised. I mean I sit, I sit chastised,' I said, blinking with mock contrition.

'Well there's no need to be like that about it.'

'I've said sorry for the error of my ways and dunno know what else to say, really.'

'Well that's not the reaction I was... Why you make it sound as if I've come over to reproach you!'

'Do I. How extraordinary.'

'Well, I think I was just being communicative!' She was twirling her middle fingers slowly round each other as she enunciated this. 'Well I'm sorry you take it so badly,' she hissed at me, her face strained puce.

'Bye,' I deadpanned.

This minor *contretemps* left me a little unsettled. Even though my complainant's complaint was probably just an excuse to sniff me over, it had interrupted my mind in its process of circling around the burning question of the existence of material evidence for BF's interest in me.

One fine Spring day three years ago, we were all having lunch in the Senior Common Room, BF's whole department sat round the table. During a brief hiatus in the chit-chat, BF casually mentioned how he hated dust-mites. He said this twice and paused.

'I hate those dust-mites,' he said in his quiet, even-toned way for a third time. Silence. Perhaps they were all too aware of the insidious resonance of the subject to trust themselves to respond to their Boss's conversational gambit. Everyone seemed to become absorbed in taking as small a mouthful of food as possible and judiciously chewing it the requisite number of times, as per medical advice, before swallowing. I put my cutlery down and glanced to the right, towards BF. The seat between us was empty, having been recently vacated by a table-hopper.

'The way I see them dust-mites...' I trailed off to see if he'd caught my drift. He lowered his head briefly to indicate his listening. 'The way I see them dust-mites is that I'm in the position of giving them houseroom.' I continued more boldly. 'I'm just providing this other life-form with shelter. I think you should take a wider view and see it as an extension of your ecological network, as t'were.'

'Like council flats?' BF said.

During this exchange the silence round the table had tautened. Then Irwin, who was sat opposite, piped up:

'Pudding, Lydia?' He smirked at me knowingly.

'Why? What have they got? Have they got anything interesting d'you think? Guess I should go see for myself.' I stood, empty plate in hand. Thinking I might as well make myself useful, I asked Irwin if I could clear his plate for him. He ceded it with a nod and I stacked it on top of mine. I'd just deposit the dirty dishes then have a quick scout round at the afters. To reach the food counter I had to pass behind BF. I briefly admired the back of his head with the shapely skull visible under close-cropped grey hair. There was something about the angle of his head and his neck that drew me.

I slid the plates onto the trolley and, swivelling on my sandaled heel to face the food counter, I suddenly knew this heel to be closely monitored by a laser-like beam of concentration. It gave me pause, right foot flexed on its bare heel as I stood there, pretending to consider the desserts, before pivoting round to return to the table.

'Nah,' I pronounced. 'Nothing worth risking the calories for.' I gave a little shrug and thought so that's that. Something in the periphery of my right side made me look down towards the floor. And there, planted a mere millimetre away from my right foot, was his left one. How could that be? Along with sheer astonishment there was a rush of monumental rage which made me immediately look away from the offending article: a large, brown-leather shod foot oh so casually plonked practically within touching distance of my heel, pointing at it like a fucking arrow. Along with astonished outrage, I was consumed by curiosity. I glanced back down and saw his big toe, planted as it was at an exact right angle to my heel. Casual my foot, this was deliberate provocation! The geometry of its placement both dispelled my fury and increased my amazement and my eyes traced the length of his leg, just to double-check that the encroaching foot did actually stem from the Professor of Graphic Design. I saw that, in order to conceal what was going on from his colleagues across the table, the posture entailed an unlikely torquing of the waist, as if he'd slyly twisted himself into one big question mark.

I tilted the stem of my glass and drained it of wine as I committed the scene to memory. If it is true that tomorrow some miraculous event may occur then what does that mean today, now, in this moment? Either the miracle will occur, in which case my present sense it may not is unfounded. Or, it does not and my present sense it could do so is mistaken and my grasp of this moment, untrue.

A Short Story About a Short Film

- Ashley Stokes -

Exterior[1]. Night. We TRACK across rows of windows and the white façade of a vast Soviet-style apartment block[2]. We glimpse living rooms and stupefied-looking people. We ZOOM in on a window to the left, then WHIP to a central

---

[1] So, first things first, Lucile. Ease yourself into your seat. Get comfortable. Slip off your heels. We're the only ones here, so you can slurp your Diet Fanta and scoff a packet of M&Ms as big as a boxer's punch bag without disturbing any snoggers or cineastes. You don't even have to turn off your mobile and can text your mates throughout the whole film if you like. I hope you don't, though. Because look, up there, moving and flickering, with its soundtrack and dialogue and beautiful black and white print. We did it. We made it. We finally finished it. Or, to be more precise, I did. I made it. It may have taken two and a half years but I did make our film, Lucile, the film that on our first date I promised you we'd make. You remember our film, Lucile? No? Really? You do, surely. It must all be flooding back to you now. Our first collaboration. Our shot at fame. This screening is just for you. Welcome to our private cinema. Enjoy your personalized director's commentary.

[2] OK, as you know, we never did raise the money to go East, let alone get permission to film there. Amberley Terrace, your old halls of residence, does have a brutalist, megalithic quality. Your suggestion that we use it as the principal location was your outstanding contribution to the production.

163

window[3]. We look down into an apartment from a stilted
angle. Snow[4] flutters around the window casement.

Inside is a BEAUTIFUL WOMAN. She is young (20s), dark-
haired and beautiful even from a distance. She folds her
arms and taps her feet on a rug, as if anxious that
someone has not yet arrived[5].

Interior. Pokey Room. Night. CLOSE-UP of a GRIZZLED MAN[6]
(late 20s) using binoculars. His elbows rest on a bulky
desk pushed against a window. A camera with a long lens
lies on the tabletop. An angle-poise lamp in the
foreground causes both his outline and a pile of notebooks

---

[3] 414 Amberley Terrace. Your old room before you met me. To my knowledge, and my knowledge comes mainly from our pillow talk, though I can't say that I've not dug a little deeper since, the list of people known to have slept here includes: Ben Sprake, Carlos Paine, Olaf Godalminger, Dirty Cheryl, Benedict 'Eggs' Rache, Hoggsy Hogg, Stu, Latvian Chemist Man with Overcoat Worn on Shoulders for Most Efficient Circulation of Air, Dr. Torquil Mizer, Armistead 'Lamby' Shanks, Joz Bovrille, Martin Bock and Specialneedsbi (I suppose you've also forgotten that Specialneedsbi played a significant part in getting us together in the first place). Otherwise, despite staring at it through a lens on and off for two and half years, I can't imagine the inside of 414 Amberley Terrace, or what went on there.

[4] And, of course, it wouldn't snow when we wanted it to snow, and Andre Font-Lackstone's uncle who works at Pinewood never actually delivered that snow machine, so our weather effects were achieved by cunning use of grated polystyrene scattered in front of the camera. The Font's acquisition of the snow machine was supposed to be his contribution to Fernfont Films, mine being the purchase of the camera used throughout. One thing I have learned is that a film as ambitious as ours quickly eats into an inheritance.

[5] This is you how I want to remember you. On the night that we met you were working behind the bar of the Flensborough Theatre. We, the old Film Studies posse, came out for a crafty one during the intermission (budget performance of *Look Back in Anger*) and there you were, demure and flustered in your serving wench mode. Specialneedsbi was slumped at the bar in his stove pipe hat and the black and yellow hooped jumper that made him look like a Colorado beetle. He was muttering and flashing his arms around, saying things about your mother that I'd probably agree with now. He was so drunk it was simplicity itself to take him out onto the terrace and dump him there. You were so relieved when I returned, so appreciative. That's when you asked me what I do. And I, rarely this suave, said I'd tell you when I met you for a drink. I got the line from a film. Stole it.

[6] Sergei Brodin, who is not actually Russian. His parents were *Socialist Worker* types from Colindale. I often lie awake at night and wonder what would have happened if I'd not cast Sergei and followed my instinct and played the part myself.

on the desk to cast mountainous shadows on the bare wall
behind him. He grimaces and adjusts the binoculars.

The Beautiful Woman paces,[7] her back to us, and holds up
the hem of her dress.

We PULL BACK to see her through the window, dancing on her
own as if to music that we cannot hear. We see her through
two overlapping circles, as if using binoculars. We hear a
doorbell ring. There is a BLUR for a second.

The Grizzled Man puts down his binoculars. He is shivering
and lights a cigarette. He stands up, but still stares at
the window as if hardly able to contain some impossible
longing. FADE TO BLACK.

Run titles.

---

[7] And there you go, Lucile, pacing that room (not actually 414 Amberley Terrace for the close-ups; that's The Font's ground floor flat in Peat Cutter Street) in the same way that you paced up and down outside the Stray Cat Café as you waited for me. I was late when I am never late. In fact, I wasn't late. I was in the Jar and Pocket opposite, keeping a sneaky look-out, checking to see if you actually turned up. I skipped out the back way and sauntered around the corner towards you, swinging my brolly and whistling a happy tune. Inside, we sat at one of those heavy wooden tables enclosed by a wrought-iron frame. We drank coffee, then red wine. You thanked me for saving you. Specialneedsbi was hassling you, you said, been at it for weeks. You didn't say why, of course. You told me then that you were an actress, just passing time behind that bar, waiting for your breakthrough. Since drama school, this recession, paucity of roles, yadda bla bla. You felt like an enclave behind that bar. 'Enclave or exclave?' I said. 'Are you an enclave, smothered by the masses, or are you an exclave, away from the flock?' You didn't answer, just smiled. Nor did I get very far with my next question: what are your favourite exclaves? Mine: Cabinda, Oecussi-Ambeno and Kaliningrad Oblast. The latter is my favourite, a little nub of Russia squeezed out onto the Baltic between Poland and Lithuania, once the capital of Old Prussia, then East Prussia, formerly Königsburg, city of Kant and annexed by the Soviet Union at the end of World War Two. I had always wanted to live there. In photos it looks pretty similar to my hometown, the place I liked to call Slutsk, a sprawl of concrete blocks separated from Mother Russia by geographic and temporal accident. I then told you how I worship East European cinema and films from the former USSR, love a bit of snow and bleakness. *A Short Film about This. A Short Film about That.* Lots of following and longing. Tarkovsky. Kieslowski. It was then that you asked me what I do.

Selina Hackett   **Merlin Prebble[8]**

Kaliningrad[9]

Screenplay by Lloyd Fernery and[10] Lucile Delph
Directed by Lloyd Fernery

Exterior. Day. Overhead shot of the communal entrance of
an apartment block. Three concrete pathways meet at the
foot of the steps, segmenting a patchy lawn[11]. The
Beautiful Woman exits the building wearing a trench coat.

---

[8] i.e., not you. You'll get yours at the end, in more ways than one. And not Sergei either, for reasons that I will reveal in good time if, that is, you still can't work this one out for yourself.

[9] 'I write and direct films,' I said. That's what I told you in the Stray Cat Café. I was sure that an electric current passed between us then. Later, sauntering through the town that I like to call Nurmansk on a night that winced with an enigmatic *Last Year in Marienbad*–ish atmosphere, your hand dangled perilously close to mine and you first articulated the idea that had already transfigured me but I was too cautious to share. We should write a film together! A film that I could direct and you could star! It would make us. It would give we two poor bedraggled graduates something to do on our own. Otherwise we would soon be found playing cardboard violins on street corners for copper coins, pleading 'what will become of us?' in mouse-like voices. I came up with a plot in a flash. During a sojourn in the Bar Zurich I scribbled out a treatment on the backs of four tourist information leaflets for a shire horse centre near the hamlet I refer to as Lersk. *Kaliningrad*. A love story. Surveillance and guilt. Escape and passion. We could go there and make it. We could go there and fall in love. You were up for all of that, you said, especially the starring in a film part. Soon afterwards, in between your shifts at the Flensborough we would meet at my flat on Red Stallion Street. You would sit on the bed and chip-in while I typed. Best moments of my life. You with your mahogany-coloured hair styled like a forties film star, your tea dance dresses in muted colours, your Mary Jane shoes, your schoolgirl slang, a string of pearls, a subtle hint of cleavage. That night the songs of Vadim Kozin overcame us and we found ourselves rolling around the floorboards and pulling off our clothes. We were like Marilyn and Miller but from colder places and more pressurized times. That was the joke we shared, how it was between us, until we began to assemble the cast and the crew.

[10] Notice the use of 'and' here, not the ampersand. In screenplay etiquette, this means not a true collaboration but that the second writer played only a MINOR PART.

[11] Back of skanky flats near the recycling centre in Nurmask, filmed from roof. The Font got bitten by a dog called Kanye and we were chased away by marauding anarcho-chavs, hence the slight camera wobble.

Seven or eight of the apartment blocks[12] stand behind her as she walks towards us along a concrete path. It is clearly freezing.

She stops, as if unsettled. This close up she's incredibly pretty, with rosebud lips and smokey eyes, the sort of girl you might only encounter once in your life. She walks right through us. FADE TO BLACK.

At the top of the path stands the Grizzled Man, tall and pale.

Exterior. Market[13]. From behind we see the Beautiful Woman saunter through a concrete precinct laid out with market stalls. The stalls are manned by burly types but there is hardly any produce. Low mist hangs and creeps[14].

The Grizzled Man furtively trails the Beautiful Woman on the other side of the stalls, smoking.

Exterior. Cafeteria called Automatik[15]. Day.

Interior. Automatik. It is a spare place with round plastic tables[16]. The Beautiful Woman sits at a window table. She is in mid-conversation with A MIDDLE-AGED MAN IN A SHABBY SUIT[17]. She laughs. The Middle-Aged Man lights her cigarette. He leans over and whispers something in her ear.

---

12 Actually what remains of the Pump House estate in Kroykov, near Slutsk.

13 That precinct near the bus station, the part of Nurmansk that's like downtown Tirana and has its own weather system so it's permanently overcast and spitting with mineral brown rain.

14 Courtesy of smoke machine borrowed from Nurmansk's third best goth metal band, Funeral in Carpathia.

15 Inventive use of the laundrette on Builder's Row.

16 All Bar One in Slutsk with the lights down low. A mate from school works there and let us in. The Font was seriously underwhelmed by the wine list.

17 I didn't tell you this at the time but I always had Dr Torquil Mizer in mind when I wrote this part. I found out later that you still only achieved a lower second class degree.

We PULL AWAY to reveal the Grizzled Man leaning against a concrete pillar, smoking. From over the shoulder of his overcoat we see the Beautiful Woman almost skip from the Automatik. The Grizzled Man lights another cigarette. Mist coils behind him.

Exterior. Vast Concrete Expanse[18]. From above, we see the Beautiful Woman striding diagonally. We linger until the tip of her shadow vanishes. The Grizzled Man follows it.

Exterior of giant office building like something out of *Metropolis*[19]. The Beautiful Woman saunters up a flight of steps. She disappears into the building.

Interior. Hanger-sized office[20]. Rows of girls are typing, making a clattery racket. The Beautiful Woman finds her

---

[18] Carpark near the medical centre at the University of Nurmansk. Filmed by me while waiting for The Font to have treatment for dog bite and sprained ankle sustained while escaping the Death's Head Legion of the Erridge Park West Anarcho-Chavs.

[19] The façade of the now disused Platinum House in Kroykov filmed from an oblique angle so it doesn't quite look so much like a pile of fifty pence pieces made out of concrete slabs.

[20] The inside of the Platinum. That's why it looks a bit damp and disordered. We couldn't lift the old coffee machine and had to cover it with a sheet. That's why it looks as if a fat ghost is frozen in the corner of the shot (something that will surely crop up in cable TV *Yuri Gellar's Real Life Ghost Mysteries Caught on Proper Film* documentaries in the future!). I know the girls all look about thirteen. That's because they are. The guy from the Kroykov School of Speech and Drama let us down on the extras front and we had to approach the drama soc of Saint Perpetua's High School for Girls. They all looked up to you, for some reason. You and I later had an argument in Café Rouge, that night Sergei sulked at the bar on his own and The Font walked off to let us get on with it. I later found The Font with three of the Saint Perp girls in MacDonald's, telling a lie about how his uncle designed that big explosion in *Superman II*. After I prised him away from his fillet-o-fishes and we returned to Red Café, as I prefer to call it, both you and Sergei had vanished. We didn't see you again until we reconvened in Nurmansk three days later.

desk. Her face is now devoid of expression.

We PULL BACK and LINGER, as if someone else is staring and staring at the Beautiful Woman. The rhythm of her typing. The shudder of her shoulders. The tapping of her heel on the grey, grey floor.

Outside, The Grizzled Man sits on the plinth of a monumental statue of some general or strongman. He looks up, sorrowfully[21]. The giant office building LOOMS.

---

[21] And so he should look sorrowful, considering that this is Sergei's last scene. Yes, as you remember, he quit after this. Well, not quit, actually. When I finally caught up with you after the Kroykov shoot—and I know this is immature of me and doesn't fit with your idea of the Hollywood life or whatever you have read in whatever biography of whichever silver screen diva and what she was allowed to get away with on set—I had suspicions about you and Sergei. I couldn't get them out of my head. You and him. Those three days. In some caravan or something. Taking your clothes off nice and slowly. That look on your face. I didn't quite believe that you had been at your Auntie Diana's in Hastings, or that your mobile's battery had run out without you noticing. I should have believed you, I know. I could have believed you. I wanted to. But you had been staring at him and he had been staring at you since we began. Sergei did insist that it was his motivation to stare at you obsessively. I sacked him anyway. See how much I loved you, Lucile? I got rid of our leading man for you. Then, of course, we had to find another one, which proved harder than I imagined. I thought everyone would be dying to star in *Kaliningrad*. Then, given what had happened with the dog, the Death's Head Legion of the Anarcho-Chavs and still being sore about me ruining his chances with the St Perps girls, The Font refused to reshoot the film again with a new actor. He assured me that no one would notice if we just carried on with a different lead in the second half. It's, like, he said, a comment on the shifting sands of identity and life in a police state where people disappear and reappear all the time.

Exterior. Dingy Bar called Eighteenth Brumaire[22]. Day.

---

[22] If you remember it was about this time that things started to get tricky. While we looked for a second Grizzled Man, we obviously couldn't continue with the film beyond shooting hours of footage of the ugliest buildings in Nurmansk. I even had to go fishing in your old drama school pond for a new Grizzled. Ben Sprake and Carlos Paine both turned me down but it was a close thing with Eggs Benedict. For about a week I thought he'd commit and told myself I could handle him joining us. Eventually, though, I had no option but to cast Specialneedsbi. A sober Merlin Prebble (he'll always be Special to me; slips of the tongue, both by myself and The Font would cause a little on-set tension later) was fresh from his life-affirming stint as an extra in a soft drink advert in which he'd pranced about in a maroon hoodie alongside a youth with cockatoo-like hair spouting vaguely sexist lifestyle statements. The experience had helped him get over you, he said. And at least, unlike Sergei, he was definitely your ex. I was raring to go but a hitch occurred when Special went all Christian Bale on me. He needed to inhabit the part, he said, and decamped for three months to stare at a concrete office block in the town I like to think of as Mordski. It was during this interlude that you started to get restless, didn't you, Lucile? You started to moan about the screenplay. Saying it was static. Saying it was boring and nothing happened. Saying that it was taking too long to get anywhere. This surprised me, because while we were writing the screenplay (note the *we*; you can hardly accuse me of foisting it on you) you raised none of these objections and seemed more concerned that the writing made you seem not just stunning but also smart *and* imaginative *and* good in bed *and* funny. Maybe this was it. Maybe I failed on the last score. I did make her the prettiest girl in Kaliningrad; I made her look intelligent *and* dreamy. But witty lines and comic banter are not my forte and perhaps—I have a point I think—not quite in keeping with the whole *Kaliningrad* mood. But you wanted another writer brought in during the hiatus. OK, anything for you, my love. Enter Shoutybollocks, the performance poet with the aviator mirrored sunglasses and the flak jacket and the wrong beard (think Grover from *Sesame Street*, think Grover looming over you in the dark, Lucile, pushing your head into your pillow with his blue, furry, lipless mouth). I wish I could say that he did something more than just confirm my prejudices against performance poetry or slam or…wank, sometimes just **wank** will do…a form of light entertainment I consider the bastardized hybrid of second-rate poetry and second-rate stand-up comedy from which emerges a chimera of arse that beguiles only the impressionable and those with short attention spans (two and a half years to make *Kaliningrad*, Shouty-B; two secs to scrawl an abruptly promoted, rhyming pub joke on a beer mat and bellow it at students who would laugh at a Spetsnaz firing squad if it was billed as *Shoutybollocks's Grover Face Rhymes Tit with Shit Show*). It's not Shouty-B's fault, I suppose. It's the world that he comes from. But as that's the same world as one Lloyd Fernery, it's not an excuse, is it? Like me he was raised in the Home Counties (or The First Circle of the Mercedes Archipelago as I like to call it), educated privately (not in the Magnitogorsk School of Mining and Metallurgy) and his father is not an exiled Russian Futurist or defected SMERSH operative but the chief exec of a Dorking-based firm selling kiddies' paddling pools and plastic slides. We both have an income to fund our dreams but unlike me the man has no romantic imagination or eastern sensibility. That impresses you, Lucile? That's enough for you? You started to spend a lot of time with Shoutybollocks, editing the screenplay while I waited for the return of Specialneedsbi. Meanwhile, strangely, there was no obvious ramping up of the script's comedy value.

Interior. Eighteenth Brumaire. A face, round and overfed[23], stares out at us. PULL BACK and he is sitting at a bar, sipping from a tumbler. He is joined by the Grizzled Man[24]. The Grizzled Man flicks a note held in his fingers, as if summoning a barman. The Over-Fed Man pulls the arm down.

> THE OVER-FED MAN
> As the promised cognac is just as
> terrible as the last shipment, this
> lot is on me.

A drink is placed on the bar.

> THE GRIZZLED MAN
> Come the Revolution, come the worst
> of the cognac.

> THE OVER-FED MAN
> When you come up with results, you
> can have what the capitalists drink.
> What have you got for me Vostok[25]?

> VOSTOK
> Impatience, Limski, is the sign of a
> narrow man.

---

[23] I'd always thought of Martin Bock when I was writing this part. He was operating the de-heading machine in a turkey factory when I asked him to audition. I like to think that I gave him his break.

[24] And there we have it. That's not Sergei. It's the far less grizzled Merlin 'Specialneedsbi' Prebble. Don't fret, Lucile. No one will notice the change. It happens in other soap operas all the time. And before you get all snarky and accuse me of using cruel and inappropriate language, you first called him Specialneedsbi, because this would-be actor and ex-fling fodder of yours 'thinks he's special and is in great need' (your words in the Stray Cat). I won't here also remind you of what you said about Davros-Street Hawk, the bloke in the invalid carriage who kept spinning into shot like a bumper car struck by lightning when we were filming at the market.

[25] Ah, so his name is revealed. Named by me after another of my favourite places, another place I'll never visit. Lake Vostok in Antarctica, a vast body of pure water sealed under the ice for millions of years. Understand the symbolism? See why I'd be drawn to such a place? Why I would identify with it?

He hands over a large envelope. Limski eagerly takes out the contents.

INSERT of big glossy black and white pictures of the Beautiful Woman doing routine things.

Limski takes the sheaf of photographs and SLAPS them across Vostok's chest.

>   LIMSKI
>   I must know. Everything. Everything
>   about this Natasha[26]. Get it all, or
>   the March of History marches over
>   you.

FADE TO BLACK[27].

---

[26] And that's her name. Natasha. You chose it. Compared to Vostok, though, it's a spanking great cliché. Couldn't you have done any better? Don't you know any other Russian names?

[27] The last straw snapped for me after we shot this scene. Let's go back over the end, just so we're clear, so there are no disputes about the facts. I'll cut all the times that you appeared not to be talking to me on set. I'll cut all the times that you failed to show up at Red Stallion Street or appeared really, really late and drunk and just fell into bed and started to snore. I won't mention your giggling at texts sent by someone who I suspect was *him*. Let's whip to that Fernfont Films production meeting at your house. I let myself in. I had bought free trade coffee and pastries for one and all. You were still upstairs, the bedroom door shut. Considerately, I let you sleep. The others arrived. The Font put his laptop on the kitchen table. Special and Martin rocked up. We were supposed to be going over the revised script. We sat there for an hour watching Special practise his spy face. The bumps and creaks started upstairs. Then down you came, your hair a mess, wearing only leggings and a T-shirt, and poured yourself a mug of the coffee that I had considerately brewed. You were shortly followed by a barefoot Bollocks, all tousled and satiated. The two of you snuggled up together at the table and drank out of the same mug. When you peered over at me through slitty eyes and then turned away, I knew it was the end of us and the end of *Kaliningrad*. It was considerate of me not to put the cafetiere through Bollocks's head. It was considerate of me not to shove a Maison Brun croissant up his khyber. It was considerate of me only to shout at you in the street.

Exterior[28]. The Window of Natasha's Apartment. Night. A
small table with chairs has been pulled into the middle of
the room. There is a chessboard on the table. Natasha[29] and

---

[28] Maybe a disruption of some sort is obvious in the final cut, given that the old Natasha disappears and is replaced by another actress (though I hope this has an effect similar to that in *Chungking Express* where the audience is not sure if a new narrative has started half way through because the direction is so intentionally enigmatic and cerebral). I can't say I knew what to do after you left. I wandered around parks and smoked like a zoo animal. I couldn't sleep. I couldn't get you out of my head. I was like a writer. I was like a writer in the fifties or sixties. I was like a writer lost in Europe somewhere. I was like a writer sodden with gin, wandering up and down the Karl Marx Allee trying to get *that* girl out his head. I was like Holly Martins in *The Third Man*, just a hack writer who drinks too much and falls in love with girls. Lucile had left me. *Kaliningrad* was not to be. *Kaliningrad* had been recaptured by the Nazis. This went on for three months that felt like years. Beautiful things—movies, snowflakes, breasts—seemed acid to me. My friends tried to console me. I sat up one night with Special and Martin and we all agreed what a beguilingly fickle thing you are and wished a plague on the house of Shoutybollocks and his couplets of toss. The film was still dead though, the film was over. I tried to write another screenplay about a writer wandering up and down the Karl Marx Allee in the fifties or sixties trying to get *that* girl out his head but it petered out. I ate a lot of pizza. I cried. I went to the doctor and asked for a cure for heartbreak. Meanwhile, The Font, bless him, was out every day, filming hours and hours of background footage of shops, concrete and manky patches of lawn (thirty hours, in fact; turned out to be bastard to edit). Special was still in so deep that he was practically inseparable from Vostok (recently, Martin said that it's hard to see him ever having a normal life now). Somehow, somehow, I regathered myself. It struck me that I'd not only lost you I'd let down my collaborators. I was depriving The Font of his first film and Special of his first leading role. I knew I could make Martin a star as well. The Phoenix Kaliningrad was born. This was where we stormed the Winter Palace. Enter Selina.

[29] And there she is: Selina. Recasting Natasha proved as difficult and forced a similar delay to the replacement of Sergei's Vostok. Two bloody months. Two months of looking at disinterested, talentless waitress-cum-actresses (though from my perspective that sentence could as well sum up our relationship, Lucile). Then, suddenly, like thunder that signals the end of an arid spell, she smashed into our lives. Selina Hackett. Sister of Miles Hackett who The Font knew from his foundation course in Bournemouth, the self-same Miles Hackett who received a two-year suspended for stealing three suitcases and a set of skis from a baggage carousel at Lutonov Airport. We didn't hold that against the sister (and they were my skis!). We thought of her as a lifesaver, a lady of the lamp come to rescue our dreams. You will notice however, that she's quite a petite thing, and given your height and presence, this scene makes it look like Natasha has shrunk in the wash. Moreover, unlike you and Natasha, Selina is blonde. We had to dye her hair. It kind of works in black and white but her hair is much straighter than yours and lacks that tendrilly, wispy thing that you've got going on. Her hair was quite a bit shorter as well, more of a bob really. Anyway, here she is, her first scene (I know she still looks nervous, as if playing chess with Weed is a Room 101 job but we couldn't keep reshooting; at take fourteen we had to settle).

a THIN MAN[30] are playing chess, studiously, not talking or laughing. There is a BLUR. The concentric circles of the binocular lenses return.

Interior. Vostok's Apartment. He puts down the binoculars and reaches for one of his notebooks.

Through the window, we see the Thin Man take Natasha's White Queen. She throws a huff and swipes the pieces from the board[31].

In profile, Vostok's pencil is looping and angling all over the page of the notebook.

Natasha, smiling now, saunters towards the window. She seems to pause and peer out into the darkness. She pulls the curtains with an abrupt swish[32].

Vostok stands and rips the page from his notebook with the same abrupt, precise gesture that she used on her curtains. He reaches out and sticks the page to the window.

---

[30] A dead-ringer, I think, for the Latvian Chemist with Overcoat Worn on Shoulders for Most Efficient Circulation of Air. I did try to track him down and cast him for this cameo, but according to Martin he'd gone back to Latvia to do paid and rewarding work.

[31] Not in the script. I think Selina had some sort of minor panic attack.

[32] This is where I think she first got it right and radiates the Natasha Effect. When we were filming this through The Font's bedroom window I felt like Vostok. Looking at Natasha but not being able to get to her. Looking at you, I mean Natasha, and finding a gulf between us. I began to realize that just like old Alfred had his Hitchcock blondes, in the future there will certainly come into critical parlance a distinct type of lady called the Fernery Brunette. I had a little tête-à-tête with Selina after this scene. I flattered her in the direction of the Stray Cat (not trying to relive anything, Lucile, you understand). I'd like to be able to say that it was as simple as two bottles of very good Shiraz and one thing leading to another. It was actually a case of two very good bottles of Shiraz drunk by me and a lunge into withdrawing arms. Outside, in that little square, where a classic half-moon hung above the ice cream kiosk, Selina explained to me that she was too professional and focussed on the role to get involved with anyone on set. Natasha is a mystery, her activities inscrutable. She must be like that. She must become Natasha. Full of respect, I walked home and must admit I had a cry, not sure over whom. It became clear soon afterwards that Martin was already giving Natasha II the benefit.

174

Interior. Supermarket[33]. Day. Natasha browses an aisle. It is lit by overhead lamps. The shelves are mostly empty. She carries a string bag with onions in it. She pauses to examine turnips. Behind her, at the end of the aisle, Vostok, camera raised, nips out and takes a photograph.

Natasha stands in the queue for the till with blank, unfathomable expression and a glass bottle of rank-looking soft drink under her arm. Vostok is behind her.

Exterior. City Square. Day. Natasha[34], string bag at her side, walks across a concrete square. Drunken lads[35] sprawl around a rubbish fountain, swigging from bottles. She stops when the lads start to jeer. They stand up and menace her. She drops her bags and her onions roll all over the paving.

Vostok jogs over. His presence scatters the drunks.

Natasha is a little flustered. Vostok collects the onions and returns the string bag to her.

                         NATASHA
          Thank you. And what is it that you
          do?

                         VOSTOK
          I work in one of these shops. 'Are
          you OK? Would you like to come and
          sit down?'

Natasha looks disappointed.

---

[33] Filmed 5am Happy Shopper, Bolingbroke Road. Turnips and onions courtesy of farm shop in Lersk.

[34] Whoops, that's actually you, Lucile, not Selina, as this bit was filmed in Tirana market after the earlier scene. That flicker in the lower right of the frame is the invalid carriage of Street Hawk flashing into shot.

[35] Navi's mates (paid in lager and the onions).

                    NATASHA
        No, I am fine. I go home now.

                    VOSTOK
        Maybe you would like a game of chess
        sometime?

Natasha laughs politely and walks away.

Exterior. The Window of Natasha's Apartment. Night.
Natasha sits on her chair again. An EFFETE MAN[36] appears to
be reading something to her from a book as he circles her
chair.

Interior. Vostok's Apartment. He has the binoculars in one
hand and is writing something in a notebook with the
other.

Natasha creases over laughing, forcing the Effete Man to
pause his reading.

Vostok, leaning back in his chair, scribbles furiously in
his book.

Natasha jumps up gleefully and rips a page from the Effete
Man's book. She holds it high in the air. He reaches up,
trying to retrieve it. She laughs and spins around like a
schoolgirl playing a game. She sticks the page on the
window.

Vostok, now kneeling forwards on his desk, pushes the
binoculars to the window, clearly trying to read what's on
the paper Natasha has stuck to the pane

Exterior. Window of Natasha's Apartment. Behind the paper
stuck to the window, Natasha and Effete-Looking jostle.
It's impossible to tell if they are play-fighting,
actually fighting, remonstrating or in the throes of love.

---

[36] This is Stanislaw Pantz, half-Australian, half-Transylvanian and the part-time librarian at
the Nurmansk Film Archive. I couldn't get anyone else. He's not a great actor but he's
certainly effete. If you study Selina's face you can see that she's clearly terrified of him.

Vostok has set aside the binoculars and has pressed his face and hands to the window. He looks like he wants to glide through the glass and float across to her.

Exterior. Window of Natasha's Apartment. She approaches the window, her expression neutral. She briskly pulls the curtains.

Vostok sits at his desk, staring into space, smoking[37].

Exterior. Street. Night. From behind, we see Natasha strolling between low-slung, oblong apartment blocks[38].

Exterior. Deserted Tram Stop[39]. Night. Natasha waits in a cone of white light thrown by a street lamp. We PULL BACK, watching her from a distance now. A tram arrives, rattling and groaning, then obscures her.

---

[37] What happened during and after the filming of this scene is still open to interpretation. Selina was so shaken up by Stanislaw (the rumours did turn out to be false, as you know) that Martin insisted on taking her 'somewhere safe' as soon as I wrapped. He draped a trench coat over her head and hurried her away before I could even shout, 'the brewskis are on me!' Otherwise pleased with the night's work, The Font, Special, Stanislaw and I decamped to Tiger Tiger for promised brewskis. Until this point, I'd been feeling great. Lloyd Fernery was back, wielding the megaphone, making art, forging a rapport with the actors. Then across the seating area I saw you, your bare shoulders, your black dress, that flick of your hair. Opposite you was Shoutybollocks, who had slipped off one of his flip flops. His bony foot was pressed on your shoe and his toe ring glistened down there in the dark. Too vividly it reminded me of the scene at the end of Bertolucci's *The Conformist* where the assumed-dead pederast is revealed to be alive and about to seduce an innocent and hungry young boy in a colonnade. I was sick, Lucile, physically sick. Hurled my guts in the washroom of Tiger Tiger in Nurmansk.

[38] Selina looking terrified as she walks through the Larkton Estate. I wanted 'imperious and frosty' and kept whispering 'Catherine the Great, Catherine the Great' to gee her up. This only made matters worse and caused S to dash for the nearest pub— The Boxer's Brace— where we found her cowering in the ladies, muttering 'not the horses' over and over again.

[39] I know. It is that bus stop where Hot Black Avenue meets Little Mullard Street. Be quiet. Don't break the spell for the others.

Natasha moves towards us up the aisle of the tram[40]. When she swerves out of shot to sit down, we see Vostok in a Breton cap and upturned collar following through the tram.

Exterior. Another Deserted Tram Stop[41]. Night. The tram pulls away from what appears to be a more suburban and less concrete-infested place.

Exterior. Leafy Lane[42]. Night. Natasha walks. Owls hoot. Gravel crunches. We PULL BACK to see Vostok tailing her at a discreet distance.

Exterior. Mysterious Lakeside Villa[43]. Night. Natasha approaches a MYSTERIOUS VILLA with pillars and statuary. Mist seemingly parts for her. She reaches the portico. The door opens, throwing a plank of light over the gravel. A MYSTERIOUS SMUDGE OF A MAN appears. He ushers her inside.

At the end of the driveway Vostok squints, smoking.

---

[40] Interior of semi-burnt-out coach found on heath. You can't really tell the difference in black and white.

[41] Bus stop where Hot Black Avenue meets Little Mullard Street filmed from other side.

[42] I'm sure you recognize this location, Lucile. That's the lane that leads to your parents' house in Sussex. You know when you have an image for a scene in your mind and nowhere else will do? Probably not. Filming here did cause a lot of discussion. The Font was against driving this far and hiring such expensive kit for such a short scene. I think he also thought it a bit unwise to revisit a place that although I'd only visited once provoked such potent memories. We were held up a little, I suppose, because I couldn't help creeping up to the house to check if you were back. Then your dad came out and there was an unpleasant and unnecessary exchange of words. The police were called because of the lights in the woods and Selina started to cry when she thought she saw a badger with skeletal paws writhing in a ditch. The footage we filmed here, I agree, is a bit unsteady and *Blair Witch Project*. I'm glad we made the effort, though.

[43] Actually Font-Lackstone's family home out near Piltdown (where they once faked the missing link). We went there after the Leafy Lane Debacle. We all slept in this huge lounge. We were like a proper film crew, all in it together, and Red Army-style camaraderie broke out as cast and crew mingled freely. Except for Martin and Selina, who slept upstairs, and The Font, who retired to his old bedroom. Special and I had a right old bonding conference. This went on for some time, until we found that all the bottles were empty and we were shouting at the tops of our voices (about who I cannot conceive) and Mrs Font-Lackstone appeared in the world's least fetching nightdress and told us that she was 'getting jolly annoyed'.

Interior. Nightclub[44]. Vostok sits alone at a table, many empty beer bottles and tumblers at his elbows. He is clearly disinterested in any of the other women here, oblivious to their Aeroflot uniform-style clothes and bouffants[45].

Interior. Eighteenth Brumaire. Day. Vostok and Limski in profile at a window table. Vostok knocks back a cognac. Limski knocks back a cognac. Vostok lights a cigarette.

Limski lights a cigarette. Vostok takes out another big envelope. Limski removes, then fingers the prints.

INSERT of b&w photos of Natasha playing chess with the Thin Man and listening to the Effete Man read[46].

Limski slams his palm on the table. When a waiter rushes over, he's waved away. Limski throws his cigarette on the floor, stands up as if about to erupt, then slowly sits down again. Vostok's expression is blank, as if he's going through the motions of pretending not to know whose side he is on.

                    LIMSKI
        This is not good enough, Comrade
        Vostok. I want to know what she does.
        Understand. Does. If it is dirty, I
        want the dirty. If it is nasty, I
        want nasty.

                    VOSTOK
        I think she just plays chess. And
        sometimes she lets an imbecile read
        to her.

---

[44] *Fluids* in Slutsk.

[45] Your friends.

[46] Even without audio this is clearly the sort of wank verse that only impresses a simple-knickers jellyhead.

```
                    LIMSKI
        Do you want me to have to find out
        from her myself? You know what
        happens when I commit myself to the
        cause of information.
```

He gets up and leaves. FADE TO BLACK[47].

Interior. Vostok's Apartment. Night. He uses the
binoculars to stare out of the window.

Exterior: Natasha's Window: She sits on her chair wearing
a night gown and is maybe naked underneath. She is relaxed
and unguarded, perhaps deep in thought. It's impossible to
know if she is alone. The doorbell SCREAMS.

---

[47] I suppose you need to know that the little contretemps we had at the New Creatives Forum bunfight occurred at this point in the shoot. I am assuming that you remember it. If not, please cover your ears. I would also like to make it clear for the record that being a serious auteur I do not usually attend such events, a networking junket for local wannabes and has-beens with a bit of so-called light entertainment thrown in to make it all seem less vulgar. The Font fancied it for some reason. Special wanted to check out any 'spare muff' as he so delightfully confessed, and Martin and Selina, well, I suppose they felt rather obliged to attend if The Font was going, not that they were fishing for other opportunities or anything. Anyway, the Fernfont Films posse arrive and clique magisterially around the bar. Everyone wants to talk to me but I am studiously aloof. Soon I am in my cups. I am on great form, tossing off *bon mots* like some latter-day Orson Welles. And then something horrible happens. There, at a table in the middle of the room, I see you, you with your back to me, you with your hair and pink tube dress, you being bored to death by that parvenu Shoutybollocks. I break out in a sweat. My *oblige noblesse* kicks in. This has to stop. You need rescuing. This was my reasoning, Lucile. I honest to goodness, hand over heart thought you needed me. I drew my party into a huddle. I gave instructions. We would rush the table, encircle the Shouty-B pocket and do the Muppet dance until he fled from this ridicule. They all agreed. We rushed. We surrounded the table and put on our best mental hospital grins and dangled our arms and knees as if on strings and chanted 'Shoutybollocks, Shoutybollocks, king of piss'. I realized that maybe this was not to be my Battle of Kursk when you looked up at me and your eyes were buried in a dark deadness that I usually associate with politicians or celebrities presenting a piece to camera. Shouty-B had this whiplash sneer going on. I realized that I was alone, that the Fernfont Films gang had not followed me into the breach. They were all still at the bar, standing there, hands over their mouths, all clearly trying hard not to laugh. Then some bureaucrat-commissar woman got up on the little stage and announced her delight that Shouty-B was about to regale us with a short set of lame, rhyme-based shtick. When you clapped, you did so in my face. Shouty Bollocks was on stage, going through the motions, a monologue-dirge called *Lady in Red Crocs*. Then I found myself in an alley and had dropped my kebab and was crying because I would never now be able to eat those red cabbage strips.

Vostok's Apartment. He scribbles in the notepad,
furiously[48].

Exterior. The giant office building like something out of
Metropolis. Day. Vostok sits on the plinth of the
monumental statue of some general or strongman. He looks
up sorrowfully at the giant office building[49].

Exterior. Market. Day. Vostok is leaning against a pillar,
smoking. We PAN to reveal Natasha[50] walking through the
market.

Vostok drops his cigarette and approaches her.

>   VOSTOK
>   Hello, miss. I trust our little
>   market is safe for you today?

>   NATASHA
>   Thank you for your concern, but I am
>   in a great hurry.

>   VOSTOK
>   Would you not like to stay for a
>   cigarette and perhaps a cup of our
>   world-famous coffee?

She laughs, like she's making herself laugh to conceal
that she's scared[51].

---

[48] The upshot of the whole Muppet Dance Forum Reversal was that everyone gathered the next morning at Red Stallion Street and stood around my bed while I shivered under the covers. The Font had been nominated to tell me that cast and crew had decided that I needed a break. The burden of writing, producing and directing a project as grand as *Kaliningrad* was clearly getting to me. I had undertaken a task akin to digging the White Sea Canal single-handedly. We should have a break. We should recharge batteries, bank accounts and bravado. I agreed. I didn't see much in the way of daylight or people for a while.

[49] This scene was actually filmed earlier in Kroykov, so that's Sergei. Don't worry about it. It looks fine.

[50] And, yep, you're right, that's you. Close your eyes if you don't like it (actually, if I ever write a sequel to *Kaliningrad*, this would be its title).

[51] Selina would have been much better in this scene.

                    NATASHA
        I know what you're after.

She tries to walk off. He grabs her elbow.

                    VOSTOK
        Why don't you tell me what you're
        after?
                    NATASHA
        I'm not after anything.

                    VOSTOK
        Then tell me, why are you spreading
        yourself so thinly?

                    NATASHA
        I consider myself lucky to be so
        thin. Now, leave me be. I have
        friends. Seriously.

He lets go of her elbow and watches her saunter away. We
LINGER on his face.

Exterior[52]: The Mysterious Lakeside Villa. Early Morning. A
car stands on the drive. The front door opens. Limski
emerges, followed by two small girls who run after him and
try to pull him back. A mousy-looking woman follows and
gathers up the children. He kisses her briefly on the
cheek, slips into his car, revs the engine and drives off.

PULL BACK to reveal Vostok behind a tree, now looking
stern even for a Kaliningrader.

Exterior. The Vast Expanse of Concrete. Day. From above we
see Limski stride across, swinging a case until he
disappears. We LINGER until Vostok appears and follows
him.

---

[52] And of course, this was filmed earlier, during the Piltdown-Jolly Annoyed Adventure.
Sharpishly, I have to admit, as Mother Font wanted to see the back of Specialneedsbi and
Lloyd Fernery.

Interior. The Hanger-Sized Office. Day. Natasha[53] types amid the clatter and racket. Her fingers spider masterfully across the keyboard. She is either very bored or daydreaming deeply. We ZOOM in to her slowly, as if we are approaching her, cautiously, with intentions, with itchy fingers and an aching tongue. CLOSE-UP of her face, its radiance and allure as she smiles. It is as if someone has just turned on a light in her mind.

Interior. Pokey Room. Night. Vostok is using the binoculars.

Exterior. Window of Natasha's Apartment. The flat seems empty. It's dark. A light comes on. Natasha sashays across the window[54].

Exterior. Communal Gardens. From overhead we see the three pathways meeting at the entrance steps of the Soviet-style apartment block. Limski arrives, walking briskly. The concentric circles of the binocular lenses surround him as

---

[53] You again, not Selina. I was able to edit this stuff together during the enforced break in the proceedings which turned out to be six-months. Six months, during which The Font told me he'd used my camera to make a series of corporate videos for a company making hand cream (actually, I later found out that The Font was being economical again and had actually been sub-contracted to work on a bizarre portmanteau film called *Twenty-Eight Wanks Later* directed by the dubious local zek I like to call Stephen Polyorkokov). Martin went back to the de-heading machine and punishing fourteen hour shifts in the turkey factory in Lersk. Selina went to Spain and posted many photos of herself wearing a bikini on Facebook and Special returned to Mordski and stared at that building. I suppose I must admit that at this point I did concede that our film, Lucile, would not be completed and would remain one of those great conundrums often speculated about by critics and academics (like Cronenberg's *White Hotel* or Kubrick's *Napoleon*). I had got so far. All I needed was the end, the final sequence, the climax.

[54] Ah, I hear you sigh with relief. I hear you gasp. That's Selina. She's back. They did start again. They all returned to Lloyd Fernery to complete the masterpiece *Kaliningrad*. This is true; I did manage to reassemble cast and crew, the circumstances of which I will relay to you in good time. The first thing to notice here is that Selina, after all that time sunning herself in Barcelona, has a tan. Natasha looks suddenly dusky, more fan dance than polka. We did try to lighten S by rubbing talcum powder on her face and arms but she started to look like Kinski's *Nosferatu*. I had hoped that I wouldn't have to use Selina at all. Again, more on this topic later.

he enters the building[55].

Interior. Pokey Room. Vostok slowly puts down the
binoculars.

PULL BACK to reveal that all over the walls of the pokey
room, all over the walls that surround him are drawings of
Natasha, of her face and her hair and her body, of her
lying and sitting and standing and walking, of her clothed
and in the nude, surrounded by flowers, surrounded by
mists[56].

---

[55] How did this come about? How did I recover? It was like this. A horrible, grey afternoon and I have nothing to do so I drift into Nurmansk and in a horrible, grey bookstore I find staring out at me from the 3-for-2 table a pile of a book called *Let the Snakes Crinkle Their Heads in Death* by the writer and performance poet I like to think of as Shoutybollocks. *Let the Snakes* chronicles his rise to the top, complete with self-effacing accounts of all his early failures and unlikely seductions. "Brilliantly-observed, couplet-based mirth," it says on the jacket. Numb, feeling like a ghost haunting my own life, I was forced to purchase a copy of *Let the Snakes* because I noticed a chapter called *Making Movies*. I wedged myself into a corner of the in-store Starbucks and read very slowly Shouty-B's hilarious account of his time 'buffing up a non-budget weepy', the 'particular craziness' of which he can't re-emphasize frequently enough. It's a project that he soon realizes is 'doomed' and he's soon side-tracked by the attentions of the 'honcho's squeeze', a girl he lovingly refers to as Luce Lid (it was 'easy to get her top off'). If you've not read this worthy tract, this veritable manifesto for modern living (Shouty-B is after all, a shark evolved to swim comfortably in the shit that's left when Living is Commerce and Art is Over) I suggest you do, Lucile, and then remember that I wrote the beautiful story of *Kaliningrad* for you. I can't say that sitting in that Starbucks, reading Shouty-B's side of things was a particularly morale-boosting experience, especially his version of the Muppet Dance Forum Reversal where 'the honcho had clearly gone tonto/ but I knocked off their socks/ with *Lady in Red Crocs*'. He went on to describe how he soon afterwards 'traded Lid for another model/funnily enough a real model/love and fame for me a doddle'. Then it struck me. You and Shouty-B were no more. You were free of his grasp. Moscow and its onion domes had been saved. The Panzers ran out of fuel at the gates.

[56] On the way home that afternoon I tossed *Let the Snakes* into the river and found myself possessed by a strange energy. The scales of the snake must now have fallen from your eyes. You would come back. You were Natasha. I wrote the part for you. We could start again. Start the whole film from scratch with a consistent Natasha and me as Vostok. I even had a fantasy of kidnapping Shoutybollocks and forcing him to play Limski (the idea supplied by Kim Jong Il's habit of kidnapping actresses and directors from South Korea and having them make private films for him). I wandered the streets and thought about you. Later, I determined that I would have to track you down. A Fernery Brunette needs a constant supply of propositions after all.

Vostok, his face full of chivalrous energy, slides a
pistol from his coat pocket, holds it up to his face and
cocks it[57].

Interior. Lobby. Limski strides towards elevator doors. He
presses a button and waits.

Interior. Concrete Corridor. Vostok runs towards the
elevators.

Interior. Elevator. Limski is going up, leering.

Interior. Elevator. Vostok descends. He is looking down,
both his hands crossed over the pistol butt that is
pressed to his groin area.

Interior. Corridor. Limski knocks on a door. Natasha opens
it and lets him in.

Interior. Lobby. Vostok DASHES towards the elevator.

Interior. Living Room. Limski and Natasha embrace. His
head rests on her shoulder. Her face is hard to read. She
is maybe scared. She perhaps more lets him hold onto her
than she holds onto him.

---

[57] You know that I called you. You must have heard the messages I left on your voicemail. You didn't reply to my texts or my e-mails. I suspected that even though I'd spelt out my motive for contacting you (*Kaliningrad*, Lucile, *Kaliningrad!*) you suspected me of having less than pure intentions. I say that these things run on tramlines and that is how it should be. In any case, failing to make contact I knew that I had to see you in person. If you would just let me take you out for a skinny latte and perhaps some waffles or tapas I could explain. Adopting the role of Stasi Lloyd, I found myself drifting past your house on the off-chance that you were coming in or going out. I took to sitting in the park opposite your house. I saw nothing. I pulled up the collar of my coat and prowled around the Flensborough but you didn't seem to be working there any more. I rang your parents' number from a phone box and put down the receiver as soon as I heard your dad's voice. I listed the sort of places you liked to go (patisseries, perfumeries and boutiques) and stood around, kept watch and waited. I thought that you might even have left town, perhaps shamed by the Luce Lid thing in *Let the Snakes*, but then I did catch sight of you, drinking coffee in Red Café with Dirty Cheryl. I lost the two of you in the street and saw you whisk off in a taxi. You were around though. I saw you outside the chemist on Vantage Street but you blanked me and jogged away quickly. I knew that I was going to have to return to the front. I decided that I'd have to go to your house and knock.

Interior. Elevator Door. A strip of light emerges with Vostok slam in the middle of it. His face is pure hardman[58]. The door hisses open.

Exterior. Natasha's Window. Natasha pulls the curtains.

Interior. Corridor. Vostok, pistol lofted, KICKS-IN Natasha's door[59].

Exterior. Natasha's Window. Behind the curtains, three indeterminate figures sway, push and shove.

---

[58] It was hard to get Specialneedsbi to follow my directions and act like Jason Statham but more hard.

[59] And so there I was, Stasi Lloyd, standing on your garden path, the blood thumping at my temples, the glittery moon above me and a breeze stinging the nape of my neck. Your light was on. The curtains were drawn and behind them I could see your outline pacing up and down. I was scared, I have to admit. I was only doing this for *Kaliningrad* (this is what I kept telling myself but even I realized that I was drowning in visions of our reunion and what we would say to each other and then some caravan somewhere and you taking your clothes off nice and slowly, that look on your face). I was Vostok and in there you were Natasha. This seemed so right. I took a breath. I smoothed down my coat and was about to take the final step to the doorbell when someone called out my name. I turned. In front of me was standing Joz Bovrille. Joz, tall and primped and Jude Law-a-like, a bottle of wine wrapped in crepe paper under his arm. He was smiling, as well he might, as even I knew he'd just scored a plum role in the sure-to-be-smash hit British comedy *The Great Leap Forward* (or *Lesbian Machine Gun Nest* as I like to think of it). 'Lloyd,' he said. 'How you doing, squire?' 'Just dandy,' I said, backing away. 'What are you doing out here?' 'Nothing,' I said. 'You here to see Luce?' 'No,' I said, 'does she live here?' 'Of course she does. Come on in. We'd love to see you. Have a drink.' 'Er…you and she, you back on?' 'Between us, I'm cashing in on my success.' He winked at me, like a co-conspirator. 'I couldn't impose,' I said. 'I couldn't.' 'Lloyd…Lloyd, come back'. But I was over the road and running through the park in the night, mud splattering the tails of my coat, my head in flames.

We PULL BACK. Things darken. GUNFLASH[60].

FADE TO BLACK. PAUSE. FADE IN[61].

Exterior. Communal Gardens. From overhead we see the three pathways meeting at the entrance steps of the Soviet-style apartment block. Limski departs, walking briskly.

Exterior. Window. There is no movement within. Then: SECOND GUNFLASH.

PULL BACK from the window to reveal the whole block and then the other blocks behind the block as we PAN across the communal gardens[62], then ZOOM in on Limski, walking off

---

[60] I must admit that when I arrived home my face was sore and I felt like blowing my brains out like that Czarist officer in Franklin J Schaffner's *Nicholas and Alexandra*. I tried to console myself by thinking that we are alike, both of us always on the hunt for a leg-up to help us realize our dreams, both of us, apart from me, who never seeks, let alone gets a leg-up. In fact, it was I who had been providing everyone else with the opportunity: Special, Selina, Martin, The Font, you. I knew now that you were never going to come back to *Kaliningrad*. I felt something in me wither and crumble. I stared out of the window at the terrace opposite and the passing cars. The world seemed suddenly provincial and English. Eventually, I found myself digging out the script we had written together, or, as I ought to say, the script that I wrote while you watched me write it and dreamed your little dreams of what it was going to do for you. I realized then that I ought to have better understood our differences when one evening you told me that your favourite films were not Eastern European, snow and bleakness, Tarkovsky, Kieslowski, but *When Harry Met Sally*, *Love Actually* and *Sliding Doors* (or, as I like to think of them: *When Lloyd Shouldn't Have Met Lucile*, *No Love, Actually* and *Doors Slammed Rudely in Face*). I should not abandon my film so close to the end because of you. I sat up all night then, revising and attending to the script's climactic sequence.

[61] I rang cast and crew each in turn. I put the last of my money on the metaphorical table. They came. Selina even came back from Spain.

[62] Not a ridiculously expensive crane shot but library footage of Reading City Centre Hexagon.

into what passes for a sunset in his head[63].

Roll Credits[64].

---

[63] You notice, Lucile, that the ending has been changed since our original script. In that version, the final scene is of Vostok and Natasha, all dolled up in opulent fur coats being lovey-dovey in some Orient Express style train carriage, en route to the west, where a better life awaits them. I couldn't help feeling that this was too optimistic and untruthful. In Paris or West Berlin or wherever, Natasha would probably become an underwear model and leave Vostok for a rich banker or a singer in a German Schlager band; and Vostok would become no more than a night watchman or small-time villain's muscle. Or, Vostok would fit in perfectly in Lisbon or London but moody, never-satisfied Natasha, like Tereza in *The Unbearable Lightness of Being*, would dump him there and return to the Land of the Weak and Vostok would be forced to go back for her (perhaps this is the baseline plot of *Kaliningrad II: Close Your Eyes If You Don't Like It*). This is what I learned from you. You changed the end, so I changed the end. And I realized that my fixation with the East and all that cold and suffering and grainy films is decadent and wrong. Now I've got a new project, *Upper Volta*, based on my love of countries that keep changing their names. A man and a woman and their struggle to be free, lots of sand and clay huts, a falconer on a roof in a head scarf surveys white buildings, heat hazes, a sidewinder coils across a dune, a jeep appears on the horizon, a sickle moon sparkles and lifts.

[64] Selina Hackett has gone to better things and is now a Human Resources Officer at the same sprawling poultry business that employs Martin Boch to work a de-heading machine. Merlin 'Specialneedsbi' Prebble is still trying to emigrate to Kaliningrad. The Font is now working full time for Stephen Polyorkokov (with my camera). Sergei Brolin, I have no idea. Shoutybollocks appears on Radio Four too frequently for my liking. Joz Bovrille won a BAFTA for his role in the film I like to think of as *A Date with Yuri Andropov*. I was surprised that you were not in it, too (I hear that nothing came of you and he). I thought I did see you the other day, though, in a film called *The Stockholm Climb*, thought I saw your backside, tightly bound in a nurse's uniform, wiggling along a corridor while the lead actors walked towards the camera. There's my girl, I thought. There's Lucile. I wonder if she ever thinks of me. I wonder if she ever finds herself on some railway platform or cheap, melancholy restaurant, late at night, alone, moonglow and sleet seeping down the window, thinking of me, remembering and saying to herself, 'We'll always have Kaliningrad'.

Bleach

- Michael Baker -

Sometimes, I think there's a ghost in the box. The channels have been changing without me pressing anything. I've even sat away from the remote to make sure it's not me doing it. I've put it on the other side of the couch, in a drawer, out the window. Things flash up, too. I can't make them out. They're so quick that sometimes I'm not so sure they're there. But they are.

I called the people at the company, and I said 'what I think is happening is, I'm picking up *God* through my satellite dish. Is this possible?' They replied in one of those voices where you can't tell if it's a person or a computer, so I checked. I said 'what comes once in a minute, twice in a moment, but never in a thousand years?' The voice said 'the letter 'M'.' Then I knew it was a computer; no one is that quick.

Jeeves has been getting on my nerves recently. I call him Jeeves because he looks somewhat like a butler. He's an arachnid for the most part, with the torso of a man and paws of a polar bear. One day I walked in to the living room and he was there; I never really questioned it to be honest with you. He says he's from the moon and that he's three weeks old next Tuesday, but he said that last week. So how old is he? I've lost track. He's not old enough to drive yet, I know that. His face is difficult to describe; sometimes it looks like a clock radio, sometimes like a giant foam hand,

and at other times it looks like a question mark. But what it looks like most is a fat, spluttering vagina. His purple mouth ticks and ticks but never tocks. Never ever. If you ever say it does then you're a fucking liar. Only the right side of his face is bearded. He seems to think that he is Kevin Spacey, but I think he's more like Abraham Lincoln only with eight legs and a giant birth canal for a face. You can never tell if he's smiling. He's like the *Mona Lisa*, except that he's an anti-Semitic arachnid that bathes in spaghetti hoops and eats dog food.

He spends most of his time sitting in the corner, cursing at me under his breath and touching himself over *Thus Spake Zarathustra* and Jacqueline Wilson novels. He's also quite into his knitting. He's good at it.

I tried to confide in him once, to tell him about these problems I've been having, but he threatened to shave my head and throw me down the stairs if I didn't 'shush.' I didn't know what 'shush' meant, but I stayed very still and very quiet for at least two hours because I didn't want to anger him. He's only half my size, but he has quite the muscles on him, you see.

Jeeves doesn't really use words much. He communicates in squeals, clicks, purrs, Chinese proverbs, radio broadcasts. He must pick up transmissions from other countries because a lot of them are in foreign languages, and I struggle enough with English as it is. When he does talk I think he sounds like a mixture between Marilyn Monroe and a crying foghorn. The words he does use are often hurtful and confusing. I find words difficult to understand. Shapes are what I like. Words are too abstract, too loose. Shapes are absolute, they're sharp, precise. But what I like most about shapes is that they're clean. Jeeves is shapeless. He's dirty. Yes. Dirty. He once told me that he gave *himself* AIDS.

Jeeves and I, we don't talk often, but he writes things. At least I think it's him. I came downstairs in the early hours of the morning to find a raw chicken sat in the microwave with a dog lead fastened to it. Stuck to its back was a Post-It-note saying 'WaLK _mE'. I figured it had to be Jeeves; it was in his hand-writing. I ended up walking the damn thing round the block, just for something to do.

It's not just writing though, he draws things too. Behind the television he has painted a man, wearing a suit and holding a briefcase, staring directly into the sun. I asked Jeeves what's in the briefcase, but he responded by calling me a worthless cum receptacle and spitting on my face. Personally, I think there's a pair of sunglasses in the briefcase. That would be my guess; it's the kind of thing he'd do. He can be very pretentious.

I guess I just feel, like, detached. Yes. Detached. I can't *touch* anything. I can't *be* touched. It's as if there's an aura, a thin film wrapped around me, a second skin that prevents me from slotting comfortably into reality. Everything is distant, elusive. The walls swell and recede all the time and it just gives me a headache. They're plastered with sad faces and what appear to be inter-dimensional portals with clenched fists protruding out of them. Every time I walk into the kitchen, the kettle swears at me in a poorly impersonated Scottish accent. I don't even dare make myself a cup of tea anymore because I know he will keep shouting 'cunt' until I leave. I feel bloated, obtuse, pentagonal, alone, dissociated—other words that won't mean much to you because you aren't me. Well, you might be. I haven't decided yet.

A man at a bus stop asked me for the time today. 'I don't know,' I said. 'My clocks have all melted off the walls.' The lecherous old nigger looked me up and down as if I was on sale, so I walked away. I walked and I walked, and then I crawled for a while to change the pace. It's comforting being so close to the floor because you can't fall any further. I wonder how Jeeves can always be so miserable; he gets to crawl everywhere. I wasn't concerned about missing my bus. No. Not at all. I wasn't even waiting for one.

I haven't been getting a lot of sleep as of late. Jeeves has been humming one long continuous note through the night. Well, he claims that he hasn't, but as soon as I lay my head on the pillow it starts. It's so faint that sometimes I don't know if it's there. But it is.

When I come down the stairs he'll be sat in the sink reading *Cosmo* like usual. Last night I said to him 'if you don't stop all this, I'll call the landlord.' The expression on his face was odd, as if he was about to sneeze, but it's hard to tell since he has a vagina for a face. Did I mention that? Yes. I think I did. If I didn't then you know now. He turned to me and said 'a bird does not sing because it has an answer. It sings because it has a song.' Then he coughed up a placenta, kicked me in the shin and scuttled off screaming.

I wash my hands a lot. It's not that I want to, I just have to. My fingertips always smell of onions and I can't stand it. I don't even eat onions. The filth is on the inside, too. I can feel it. I can taste it. It can taste me as well, I'm sure.

The bottle said to avoid contact with eyes and skin, but it's not as if I have any skin on the inside. No. I wouldn't have thought so. Skin is something for show.

'IRRITANT', it said on the back. But let me tell you, there's nothing more irritating than knowing your organs are smothered in grease. No. There's nothing worse than knowing your soul is made of *shit*. There was nothing else of interest on the bottle and so I drank and drank till it seared my throat. Till it ignited in my stomach like holy fire.

When I woke up in the white room with white people wearing white, they told me that I needed help. They asked me 'what?' and 'where?' a few times, but what they asked me the most was 'why?' I told them that it flushed me out. I was clean, I told them, for the time being. I asked where Jeeves was. I thought he must have been the one who brought me in, but the expression on their faces suggested to me that he didn't.

For some reason the doctors thought I was trying to kill myself. I told them if I wanted to do *that* there are better ways. A bullet to the back of the head would be the most efficient method, the most painless—the cleanest. But the government is sadistic, I told them. Yes. Gun control forces us to be creative.

The television is at it again. I think the screen is another portal, to some distant parallel plane. Its tiny inhabitants can see me too, I'm sure of it. Attractive women offer me things for my troubles. It's nice, comforting. I'd like someone like that.

Jeeves loves the television. He'll sit there completely static in front of it for days watching *House*. He believes that it makes him more intelligent. He even demanded a C.A.T. scan after he diagnosed himself with erythropoietic protoporphyria. I told him that he wasn't making any sense. He responded by telling me that my car was being towed. Well, that really made me mad. I ran out into the street demanding justice from the postman. Then I realised that I don't own a car and I went back inside feeling rather flustered. When I returned, Jeeves was on fire, dressed in a rather tawdry Batman costume. It was all very confusing.

Last night I had an awful nightmare. It was so surreal. In the dream I woke up next to a loving wife, and we shared a small nutritional breakfast. Then I put on a suit and headed out the door to work. I worked at an office. It was bland, nondescript; a place where they processed something or other for someone. I worked from nine in the morning till five in the evening, at which point I went home to my wife and children. We watched family-friendly programming until ten, at which point my wife and I put the children to bed. We slept in our affordable, comfortable double bed in our nice house in our nice universe and everything was nice. Then we woke up again and the dream repeated itself.

I woke up screaming and even swearing. I said 'fuck.' Yes. I did, honestly. I only ever swear when I'm really worked up, or when I'm trying to impress you.

I got out of bed and I saw that an envelope had been slid under my bedroom door. On the back it said 'A_poEm'. I opened it and sure enough, there was a poem inside. It said:

> *roSeS_aRe_reD,*
> *VioLets_aRe_blUe,*
> *I'm_KevIn_SpACey,*
> *NOW_PISS_OFF.*
>
> *bY_DaPHnE.*
> *xoxo*
>
> *p.S._...cOme_DownsTairS.*
> *p.P.s._...BRiNG_mOuthWaSh.*

I walked downstairs and Jeeves was hunched over in the centre of the living room. His stomach was bloated and heaving. He was throwing up what looked like petrol and whole sticks of butter all over the floor. For a second I think he took on the form of a rainbow. I asked the freezer what was wrong with Jeeves, but it just pissed itself and giggled at me. The microwave was chanting 'three lions on the shirt' at the top of his voice, which didn't help matters. Neither did the fact that Genghis Khan was stood in there eating all of my cereal again. He's a very loud chewer. There was a human leg on the windowsill, but Jeeves said he didn't know where it came from when I asked him about it. Well actually, what he said was 'give a man a fish and you feed him for a day. Teach a man to fish and you're a meddling Marxist kike.'

My favourite room in the apartment is the bathroom. I like it because it is the only room with a lock on the door. I feel safe. Yes. Safe is how I feel when I'm in the bathroom. It is usually very clean too. However, this morning I found that Jeeves had written more of his poetry on the bathroom mirror. Normally I wouldn't have minded, in fact I encourage him to express himself, but he wrote it all in my toothpaste and now I barely have any left. My teeth have to be clean, you see. Everything does. But you know that—if you've been listening that is. Anyway, the poem went like this:

> *miRRoR_MirrOr_oN_tHe_wAll,*
> *whO_iS_tHe_fAirEst_oF_TheM_all?*
> *KevIn_SpACey_iS,*
> *NOW_PISS_OFF.*
>
> *bY_DaPHnE.*
> *xoxo*
>
> *p.S_GOD_IS_DEAD.*
> *p.P.s_WE'RE_OUT_OF_FUCKING_M-M-M-M-M-*
> *MIIIIIIIIIIILK.*

It is Christmas Day today. Well, I'm not sure if it is actually December 25ᵗʰ, but Jeeves and I decided that we'd like it to be Christmas. I bought him *Schindler's List* on DVD. He said the film was 'absolutely hilarious, a comedic masterpiece.' He gave me a sweater that he knitted himself, a peppered foreskin and a cum-sodden Chuckle Brothers poster. I was very grateful, even if it was a little crude. I said 'would you like to say grace, Jeeves?' He said 'each generation will reap what the former generation has sown.' Then he grabbed the kitchen knife and carved this poem in the Turkey:

> *ONe_tWo_tHRree_fOuR_FivE,*
> *OnCe_i_CauGHt_A_fiSh_aliVe,*
> *SiX_sEvEn_eigHT_NIne_tEn,*
> *THen_i_TolD_ iT_To_PISS_OFF.*
> *AMen.*
>
> *bY_DaPHnE.*
> *xoxo*

I have recently started working at a petrol station. My job is to stand at the till and I.D. people if they are buying alcohol, glue, razors, lighter fuel, party poppers, knives, corkscrews, fireworks, cigarettes or other fun things. I had to call in sick today because I think I'm coming down with a cold. When I close my eyes I see shapes: squares grinding against each other, circles spinning and nagging at me in droves. I asked them to leave me alone but they started spinning faster and nagging harder. Triangles are the most unchaste shapes below eight sides; all they do is fuck. When

I look in the mirror, I see someone other than myself. I even jump in from the side to catch the reflection by surprise but it's still the same. If I un-focus my eyes, I take on the form of something entirely different, like a cubist interpretation of myself, an installation, a network of unrelated components. My senses feel dull and vague and drawn out. When I undress, *O Fortuna* starts to play very loudly from my speakers (especially when they aren't plugged in), which is a little anti-climactic considering the inadequate shape of my body. I explained all of this over the phone to my doctor and the voice said 'I see' in such a cold, professional way that I knew it was another computer. No one is that clinical, not even people who work in a clinic. 'Are there voices?' it said in bleeps and whistles. 'No,' I said. 'But I'd love the company.' Then they made this noise, like a click, followed by a high-pitched ringing sound that went on for fourteen hours. Eventually I just put the phone down on them. I wasn't in the mood.

The shop at the petrol station is quite small, so I only work with one other person and that person is a girl named Sophie. There's something clean about her, something quiet. Not like Jeeves; even when he's silent he's shouting. I like the words she uses. She doesn't use the letter 'g' a lot, which is good because I hate the letter 'g.' It's so ugly and lazy and arrogant. There it is again, finding its way into my words. Prick.

I asked Jeeves what he would think if I asked Sophie out on a date. He said 'a rat who gnaws at a cat's tail invites destruction.' I don't remember anything after that. I just sort of blacked-out. I regained consciousness what must have been several hours later with Jeeves cradling me, rocking ever so gently and sobbing. On the wall in front of us it said:

> *pOLLuTed_sPRING!*
> *PoISOned_WeLL!*
> *IT's_pUrGatOry_fOR*
> *YOU.*
>
> *bY_DaPHnE.*
> *xoxo*
>
> *p.S_...I'm_KevIn_SpACey.*

I think he is jealous of the fact that I've taken a liking to Sophie. When I'm around her I feel normal. Yes. Normal. No. Not normal. I wouldn't want to be normal. But she makes me feel fine, acceptable. Yes.

Perfect how I am. She's older than Jeeves, but slightly younger than me. Unlike me, she is very attractive. Yet she still calls me 'handsome'. I've never been called that before. She always says nice things. When she speaks it's the only time that I really enjoy words. Words like 'sweet' and 'cute' and 'cashier'. They aren't like the words Jeeves uses. He takes every opportunity he can to lower my self-esteem. He always calls me 'slut', 'Bobby Davro's left testicle' and 'a cock gobbling fag-enabler.' I think he uses the letter 'g' in that last one just to make me mad. He knows me all too well. Another thing he told me is that I'm merely a figment of his imagination, which really messed with my head. I had to sit down for a few minutes after that one.

Anyway, I asked Sophie out on the date. She said 'yes.' It's true, she did. We're going to go straight after work on Friday. I'm not sure where to take her. I was thinking of a nice dinner somewhere. Somewhere fancy. Somewhere clean, of course.

Jeeves hasn't spoken much since the incident last week; I think he's depressed and probably a bit embarrassed over the whole thing. He has tried to make himself inconspicuous by wearing a ceremonial Cherokee mask, painting himself black and sitting on the ceiling, but I still know he's there. He wants to say sorry, I'm sure, but he can be very stubborn. Although earlier when I was getting all worked up trying to make my hair nice enough for Sophie, he put his paw on my shoulder and said 'a diamond with a flaw is worth more than a pebble without imperfections.' It was the nicest thing he has ever said to me.

Work was hectic today. At least three people came into the shop. One man was looking at Sophie like he wanted to do bad things to her. Yes. Illegal things. Evil things. *Unclean* things. I took him to one side and whispered in his ear that he should leave. But what I really said is that if he didn't get out I'd slash his throat like a fucking pig. He went all pink like the little piggy he was and trotted off without looking back.

I woke up in the middle of the night again to find another envelope on my bedroom floor. Like usual, a poem was inside. It said:

> *FUCKING-G-G-G-G-G*
> *WHOREWHOREWHORE*
> *WHOREWHOREWHORE*
> *WHOREWHOREWHORE*

bY_DaPHnE.
xoxo

p.S_...I love you SO much.

There's something different about Jeeves now. Yes. Something under the surface. He seems brooding, deflated, faded, temporal, hopeless—other words that won't mean much to you because you're not him. Well, you might be. I haven't decided yet. Either way, I can't live with him anymore. I told him that Sophie and I are in love, and that he is no longer welcome in our life. He said 'do not employ handsome servants,' but what he really said was nothing. No. Nothing. He was still. Just still. I left him in the dark and went back to bed.

Friday has finally come round. Sophie and I have spent the entire day talking about things. You know, stuff. You wouldn't be interested. Well, you might be. I haven't decided yet. Either way, she has said she is looking forward to our date tonight very much. I think things will be better now that Jeeves is leaving. Sophie and I can live together and she can be happy and I can be happy. We can be happy together.

It is almost eleven and so I tell Sophie to wait in the car while I lock up. She tells me to hurry and smiles in that way I don't know how before she skips outside. I walk into the cloakroom to grab my coat from the locker.

I open the door and a slip falls out onto the floor. It says:

PeTRoL_plUs
FIREworks_plUs
A_mATCh_eQUaLS
HAHAhahA_HAHA!

bY_DaPHnE.
xoxo

p.S._...noW_wE_CAn_bE_toGeTheR_FOREVERANDEV ERANDEVER.
p.P.S._...I'm_KevIn_SpACey.

Unthologists

Viccy Adams is in the final stages of a PhD in creative writing at Newcastle University, researching the intersections between novels and short story collections in contemporary British fiction. She is addicted to reading fiction, drinking tea, and scribbling notes on any paper or paper-related product close to hand when an idea comes into her head. Read/listen to more of her work or contact her via www.vsadams.co.uk.

Deborah Arnander has worked as a translator, researcher and speech-writer. She has a Postgraduate Certificate in creative writing from the University of East Anglia. She won an Escalator New Writing Award in 2009, and is currently working on her first novel, about a GI baby, set in wartime Norfolk and 90s California.

Michael Baker is nineteen years old and studying Creative Writing and English at the University of Hull. He is from Grimsby, North East Lincolnshire.

James Carter grew up in Norfolk and has lived, worked and studied in Stoke-On-Trent, London and now Norwich.

Sherilyn Connelly is a San Francisco-based writer. Her words can be found in *It's So You: 35 Women Write About Personal Expression Through Fashion and Style* and *Gender Outlaws: The Next Generation* by Seal Press, *I Do / I Don't: Queers on Marriage* by Suspect Thoughts, *Good Advice for Young Trendy People of All Ages* by Manic D Press, *More Five Minute Erotica* by Running Press, *Visible: A Femmethology, Volume Two* by Homofactus Press, and publications such as *Girlfriends, Instant City, Other Magazine, Holy Titclamps,* and *Morbid Curiosity.*

Sarah Dobbs is in her final year of a PhD in Creative Writing at Lancaster University. She works at the University Centre at Blackburn College where she is currently developing a new Joint Honours degree in Creative Writing. Her novel *Killing Daniel* is currently with Susan Yearwood and is being submitted to publishers. She's at work on her second novel, entitled The *Lemonade Girl.*

Jenni Fagan has been published in the UK, USA, India, Istanbul, NZ, Paris and Athens among others. Her debut collection *Urchin Belle* sold out in the UK last year, it is now available from Kilmog Press in New Zealand. Her collection *The Dead Queen of Bohemia* is due out soon. Jenni is currently a writer-in-residence and has just completed her novel *The Panopticon.* Her *Scold's Bridle* installation with women in prison in the UK and USA is on exhibit in London.

Mischa Hiller is author of the critically-acclaimed *Sabra Zoo.* His second novel is to be published in the spring of 2011.

Sandra Jensen was born in South Africa and presently lives in Ireland with her partner and her cat. Her work has been published in *Word Riot, Sou'Wester, AGNI* and others. Her short story manuscript *A Sort of Walking Miracle* was short listed for The Scott Prize (Salt Publishing). in 2010 she was awarded a professional writer's grant from the Canada Council for the Arts to develop her novella, *Serendip,* into a novel. When Sandra is not staring at the blank page she moderates the online writer's workshop *Diving Deeper.*

Maggie Ling has, in her various urban incarnations, been a fashion designer and illustrator, children's charity worker, children's book illustrator, cartoonist and occasional poet, her work published in books, magazines and newspapers, including the *Guardian, The Observer* and *The Independent,* a cartoon collection, *One Woman's Eye,* published by Virgin Books. Deserting London for the sunny Suffolk coast she traded drawing board for Mac and began writing fiction. Poems have since appeared in *Mslexia* and *Lines in the Sand: New Writing on War and Peace* (Frances Lincoln) and short stories shortlisted by World Wide Writers, *Mslexia* and Cinnamon Press. A novel is currently under consideration at Seren.

Melinda Moore writes literary short fiction and a comic political blog. She is married with two children, and is an ex-ballet dancer, ex-model and ex-political aide. She hopes not to become an ex-wife and ex-writer.

Martin Pond lives and works just outside Norwich, where a career in IT pays the bills. Inclusion in the *Unthology* is his first writing credit. He is currently trying to fuse a 19th Century approach to storytelling with 21st Century technology by publishing his latest work in weekly installments at drawntothedeepend.blogspot.com

C. D. Rose's work has appeared in *New Writing 14* and *Parenthesis,* and at untitledbooks.com. He has lived in Italy, France, Lebanon, Morocco and the United States, but—as yet—has never visited Latvia.

Lora Stimson lives in Norwich, where she is a lounge singer and cabaret promoter. Lora studied creative writing at Norwich School of Art & Design and at University of East Anglia and is currently a creative coordinator with Writers' Centre Norwich. She has been published in *Arts Professional, IP1* Magazine and *Ink Sweat and Tears* and has had work shortlisted for competitions with *Mslexia* and *ABC Tales.*

Ashley Stokes's first novel, *Touching the Starfish* was published by Unthank Books in 2010.

Karen Whiteson lives, teaches and writes in London. Her stories have appeared in *The Edinburgh Review* and in anthologies published by *Penguin* and *Aurora Metro.* Her play for radio was broadcast on Radio 3 and her libretti for music theatre have been performed at the ICA and the Riverside Studios. An essay on Cocteau's film *La Belle et la Bête* is due to appear in the next issue of *Artesian Magazine.*

Tessa West's career in prisons was followed by her appointment as an independent member of the Parole Board. Now retired, she can focus on writing prose and poetry. The latest of her three novels is *Companion to Owls*. Her biography of the prison reformer John Howard will be published by Waterside Press in 2011. Some years ago she cycled across Cuba, and this year along the Canal du Midi.

UNTHANK BOOKS

Touching the Starfish

- Ashley Stokes -

'Crisp, witty and scalpel-sharp, *Touching the Starfish* doesn't miss a trick in its arch depiction of the orthodoxies and absurdities of Creative Writing Programmes and the many varieties of pond-life to be found therein. It's deadly accurate too on the often hilarious miseries of the writing life.'

Lindsay Clarke

Ashley Stokes's comic masterpiece stars Nathan Flack, a writer exiled in a backwater and teaching creative writing to a group of high-maintenance cranks and fantasists. When a very literary ghost by the name of James O'Mailer starts to haunt Flack, he was to ask himself: is he sinking into a netherworld of delusion, or is he actually O'Mailer's instrument?

'The work of an anarchic imagination stuffed with incident and mordantly humorous observations.'

Eastern Daily Press

'Comic writing doesn't get better than this.'

EssentialWriters.Com

ISBN 978-0-9564223-0-9

Available from www.unthankbooks.com, The Book Depository, Amazon, Waterstones.com and all good booksellers.

www.ingramcontent.com/pod-product-compliance
Lightning Source LLC
Chambersburg PA
CBHW031101020726
47495CB00007B/1993